THE

Girlfriend Experience

K.A. Campbell

Copyright © K.A. Campbell

ISN: 0692467041

ISBN-13: 978-0692467046

DEDICATION

This book is dedicated to my four children Aminah Cottle, Ariyah Cottle, McCoy Jones, and Miriam Finch. Without these four wonderful blessings from God there would be no me. I would have no reason to strive to be a better woman each and every day. I thank God for giving such wonderful gifts in you. I'd also like to dedicate this book to my baby brother De'Angelo Lytton, R.I.H. baby boy. There isn't a day that goes by I don't think about you. I'd also like to dedicate this to my best friend, Tyauna Anthony. If you were here I know you'd be routing for me so tough. That was how we did with one another. You never turned your back on me. You always stayed a loyal and true sister until the very end. R.I.H. beautiful lady. Until we meet again. I miss you so much. Last but not least I dedicate this book to my mother. Thank you for always pushing me forward and not allowing me to remain stagnated. You are amazing Sheryl Campbell. I love you.

The Girlfriend Experience

Acknowledgments

First and foremost I have to give thanks to God for giving me this wonderful gift of writing. He has shown me so much favor and I'm grateful beyond measure. To my grandparents Russell and Sally Jones I'm so happy to be able to make the two of you proud. Thank you Yolanda Carr and Milton Carr for always being there and encouraging me along life's journey. You two are an awesome team! To Daniel Campbell and wife Allie I appreciate your support and love you dearly. To my favorite cousin Latrice Parks-Gold I love you, thank you for your support, and all that bragging. To Joe Campbell and wife Tania I love you and am happy to call you family. To Lisa Frank and husband Derek you two are amazing and so inspirational, I'm grateful to have you as spiritual mentors. To my little brothers Vonnie Jackson, Kevin Jordan, and Darrien "Debo" Dean, and my baby sister Tierra Jackson, I love you guys. I hope that one day I can inspire you all as much as you inspire me. To Corey Smith you're such an amazing friend and man. To me you're like a superhero. I thank you for being a part of my life and consistently encouraging me to be better. Last, but not least to all of my family, friends, and fans thank you for being supportive, patient, and encouraging during this journey. You don't know how much your support means to me.

CHAPTER ONE

His tongue moved rapidly over my clit as my hips followed the motion. The more I moved the more lost I became in my thoughts. My hot spot was wet, but I felt nothing. It was as if I were numb to the idea of coming. What used to be pleasurable with Ryan had just become a duty.

I'm not your typical sad story. As a matter of fact, my childhood was great. I come from a family of professionals. I wasn't abused, and never wanted for anything. However, there was always this feeling inside of me. This feeling that pushed me to be different. An urge to go out and get things on my own, unlike my siblings who'd made it their full time job to make a living off of my father's blood, sweat, and tears.

The first experience was exhilarating. I wasn't afraid, nor did I feel degraded. It wasn't like how I'd heard some of the other girls describe it to be. Instead, I felt liberated and free. I wasn't held to any standard and could totally let go and be me! And when that money hit my hands, I was hooked.

You see I wasn't your average "call girl". I was the ultimate experience. I did it all and didn't think twice about it. Having no limits was what got me the big bucks in this business. And the money was my main priority.

Growing up, I was exposed to many powerful people. We'd had doctors, lawyers, even senators, at our home regularly. I was always around the "right people". However, I'd never met anyone quite like Mr. Chastain, or shall I call him Victor? He'd been a friend of the family's for many years. He was the only one of daddy's friends that I can remember admiring since I was a little girl.

At 17 years old when I'd finally started to develop, I noticed he started to admire me as well. When he and his wife split leaving him with custody of the kids, I was more than happy to come baby sit when he needed some adult time. One night he came home a little more tipsy than usual, and what used to be fantasies about my daddy's old friend quickly became a reality.

Yes, it sounds cliché, but one thing led to another and before I knew it Victor had ripped my tight little shirt in half. He took my pink nipples into his mouth one at a time circling his tongue around them, blowing, sucking, and biting. It drove me crazy. He wasn't the first I'd ever had sex with but he was the first to ever make me cum.

The attention he paid to each of my breast was like a beautiful serenade causing my body to become tense and clammy. When he squeezed both of my breasts together suckling them simultaneously I felt as if I was in heaven. He held onto me with so much passion I believed we were the only two people on earth.

Those thoughts of Victor invaded my mind bringing feeling back into my clit. I started to moan imagining that Ryan was him. I grabbed hold of his dark brown hair pushing his face further into pussy. I was grinding hard and fast, while, his tongue flickered and probed sending volts throughout my entire body.

After he'd finished playing with my nipples he stood there staring me in the eyes. I was mesmerized. I felt as if I was floating or in a dream, but I wasn't. The squeezing of my breasts, probing of my nipples, and pressure coming from his pants threatening to stab my vagina were all real feelings.

He took his right hand and began rubbing against my panties, feeling the warmth of my juices. I followed his rhythm, waiting, hoping, and praying that he would take it further. One of my lips poked through the side of the fabric which was his queue to go for the kill. His thick index finger entered my hot spot causing me to look down. He pinched my nipple hard, forcing me to look back up.

He told me never to look away from him as he continued to move his fingers in and out of the walls that were now closing in around his fingers. I obliged as I met his every thrust with my own. I wanted to feel his manhood deep inside of me, but didn't dare ask.

He asked me what I knew about pleasuring a man. I had no answer. I didn't know anything, but I was willing to learn if he was going to teach me. I allowed those words to slide off my tongue. They seemed to pull him deeper into that lustful trance.

My legs kicked back and forth as I attempted to help him pull off my panties. The task had proven to be too much work causing him to rip them from my body. Without missing a beat, he pulled out his long thick muscle slamming it into my pussy. I let out a yelp as the pain invaded me, causing me to lose my breath. I'd never felt such a feeling. Just like that I was hooked.

Victor was how I got through my moments with Ryan. It wasn't that I didn't care about him it was just that.... Well.... He was who everyone expected me to be with. We'd been dating since high school. He was the All American boy that got a college scholarship despite his family's ability to pay for him to go to school. He planned on being a lawyer, financial analyst, CEO, or something. I couldn't even remember that was how much I cared about what he had going on.

Ryan was boring. Just something or should I say someone to do until Victor was available or I had a client. He was starting to notice my lack of availability. He'd cry and complain about me never spending time with him. I'd always blame it on my hectic school schedule. The school schedule that was actually no longer existent.

I didn't have time for school at the moment. The money and the rush of escorting brought too much "life" into my life. I never knew what I was going to get. I was living life anticipating something exciting, something dangerous, something new, every time I went out on a call.

I pulled Ryan's head away from his feast lightly kicking him in the chest. He looked up at me confused. I smiled, enjoying how I'd been keeping him on an emotional roller coaster. Mounting myself onto his penis I began to ride him hard and fast.

I rolled my eyes as he told me to slow down. I couldn't slow down even if I wanted to. I needed this sexcapade to be over with quickly. I glanced over at the clock if he didn't explode soon I'd be late for my date. Time was money and I had none to waste.

"Tawny, slow down!" Ryan insisted, using his muscles to keep me at bay. I looked down at his frustrated face with contempt. With no words in response I began to regain my momentum.

Ryan pushed me off his lap before running his fingers through his hair and letting out a loud sigh.

"What now?" I asked, clearly agitated myself. This was the perfect time to start an argument so I could get the hell out of there. Ryan looked at me shaking his head from side to side.

"What's going on with you Tawny?" he asked. I wanted to feel sorry for him but I couldn't. Maybe it was selfish of me, but he was really starting to become a nuisance in my life. I was young. I was supposed to be free to do whatever I wanted whenever I wanted to do it. Why did I have to be tied down because that was what everyone else expected?

"Listen," I said, getting up starting to slide back into my clothes. "I have to go. I really need to study." I lied.

"You know my heart tells me different," he said as his voice cracked. "I can't even tell when you're lying or telling the truth anymore." He said sounding defeated.

That got my attention. What did he mean he couldn't tell when I was lying or telling the truth? He'd had yet to confront me about any of the lies I'd been telling him.

"And what's that supposed to mean?" I asked, pretending to be offended. It was a weak attempt to turn this entire conversation around on him and make my exit.

"Dammit!" Ryan yelled, squeezing his eyes closed as he shook his head. "You're not going to turn this around on me. Not this time." He said, sounding totally exasperated.

That was my queue to go in for the kill. There was no need for us to continue going back and forth with one another. He was trying and I wasn't. I didn't care about the relationship anymore. To me it was a dead matter. To Ryan, however, he was still holding onto the ledge for dear life.

"Maybe, we should just take a break," Ryan sighed, before I could make a dramatic scene. That was music to my ears and I didn't make any attempt to change his mind about it.

"Yes, maybe we should," I agreed, slipping into my heels. I'd barely given it a second thought before opening my mouth. Ryan was a great guy and he surely didn't deserve to be treated like I was treating him, but I didn't know how else to play my cards. I'd tried to cut down on the time we spent together, phone conversations, affection, nothing seemed to work. I was relieved that he was finally getting it.

Now I could be free to do exactly what I wanted to do. None of which he was included in.

"And just like that you're going to walk out the door?" he asked with his voice cracking. I knew it was too good to be true. I knew he wouldn't allow me to just walk out of his dorm without a fight.

"What do you want me to say, Ryan?" I asked, contorting my face as if it pained me to be having that conversation with him.

"Nothing," he said, "just get out!" he shouted, throwing my purse at me, spilling all of its contents including a box of condoms out on to the floor. He reached down, picked them up then looked at me in disgust.

Snatching them out of his hands, I smacked my lips and made my way out of his room never looking back. He had managed to piss me off. That was something I wasn't expecting. I'd wanted our break up to be as smooth as possible. I never wanted to hurt him, like I said he was a sweet guy.

How many hints could a girl give him? We were 25 years old. We had our entire lives ahead of us. Why be tied down to one person constantly planning for your future? It was time to live a little!

I burst out of the building inhaling the fresh spring air. The sun was shining bright and I felt light. I glanced down at the pink diamond encrusted Rolex on my wrist. I had just enough time to make it on time. My cell phone began to buzz. I didn't have time to answer it, whoever it was I'd call them later.

I jumped in my car skidding out of the parking lot feeling free. My drive home was silent aside from all the possibilities that lie ahead of me. I loved my life and lived it on my own terms. I smiled imagining all that was to come.

When I got home, I noticed Victor's roadster had been parked inside my garage. A smile crept across my face. It was always a pleasure being in his presence. He'd turned me onto all the great things this world had to offer.

I walked into my Townhome calling out his name. He didn't answer, but I could hear him talking on the phone as I made my way upstairs. When I walked into my bedroom, he was sitting on the bed babysitting a line of coke.

"Ah, of course Mr. Schwartz, you will be more than satisfied with her services. She's an excellent girl." He smiled into the receiver. "She stands about 5'9, with long blonde hair, fair skin, and slim just how you like them. She's my most prized possession." He continued winking at me.

I smiled back at him eyeing the mirror sitting on his lap. He nodded his head as I sat down beside him, dipping my nail into the powdery substance. I leaned forward, inhaling deeply. The substance dripped down my throat, bringing me a sense of calmness, peace, as well as chaos. I smiled.

Like I said being around Victor was always a pleasure. He came with many perks. I lay next to him for a few minutes listening to him speak with Mr. Schwartz. I loved the way he presented me to our clients. Victor hung up the phone placing the glass on the nightstand.

"How was your day?" he asked, wrapping his arms around me.

"Interesting," I responded, as I closed my eyes taking in his scent.

He smacked me on my behind as he told me to hop up and get ready. I looked at him like he'd lost his mind. I still had two hours left before I met up with Alex one of my regulars.

"Change of plans beautiful," he said, noticing my apprehension. "Mr. Schwartz will be picking you up in 30 minutes." He added.

"He's picking me up from my house?" I asked, looking confused. That was the number one rule of the game. No one was supposed to know my real name or where I slept. I was a taken aback by the lack of professionalism that was coming from Victor at the moment. Pissed was not even the word to describe my mood.

"Calm down," he responded, rubbing my leg and placing a soft kiss on my forehead. That usually brought my blood pressure down a notch. "He's a personal friend of mine."

I really didn't care how close Victor and this Mr. Schwartz were, I didn't appreciate a date having my address. You could never be too sure with those guys. Several girls I knew had been in some pretty questionable situations in the past. Situations that required them to think fast on their toes and pray that security made it into the room in time to save their asses. I gave Victor half a smile before making my way to the shower. I prepared as quickly as possible, feeling in my soul that that tonight was going to be a game changer.

CHAPTER TWO

"Please don't call me Mr. Schwartz, I'd prefer Lutz," he insisted, in a strong German accent. Despite me being unsure about this man previously he'd proven to be the perfect gentlemen thus far. Usually you could tell if you were going to have a problem with a client after being with them for a little while, but this guy was just short of amazing.

I smiled pretending to be interested in what he was saying. I'd learned to do that often. Pretend. It was my job to make them think they mattered. That always guaranteed me a hefty tip.

"So, Lutz," I smiled. "I think it's important that I let you in on a little secret."

He raised an eyebrow before nodding for me to continue. He was a man of very few words and his presence screamed POWER!

"This has been one of the best dates I've been on," I laughed, causing him to smirk. I knew he didn't believe me and I wasn't offended because that came with the territory. None the less I told him because it was the truth. He made me feel comfortable and had a good spirit about him.

So I know you all are looking like *what the hell does she know about someone having a good spirit?* For those questioning my judgment, I have one name for you Mary Magdalene. I'm not a bad person I just, enjoy fucking. Any woman who's true to herself enjoys fucking too.

"I'm serious," I chuckled, making myself blush as I placed his hand in mine.

"And what makes this date so...
so.... Best?" he asked.

"Look around honey," I said, moving
my head from left to right then focusing
back on the man seated in front of me.
"This lovely dinner, you're kindness and
respect is well appreciated," I stated.
"Although we both know why I'm here, you
Mr. Schwartz have still treated me like
nothing less than a lady." I acknowledged
sincerely.

"Oh it's coming," he responded,
smiling mischievously causing my entire
body to shudder. I blew off his statement,
although I questions if I should've been
worried or not.

We had an amazing dinner,
exchanging small talk and a few laughs.
After a few drinks I'd completely forgotten
about Lutz's warning and was enjoying the
hell out of myself. It seemed that Lutz had
lightened up a whole lot too. When we
made our way inside the nightclub both of
us were going full throttle.

The music blasted as the lights
flickered on and off. There were people

everywhere jumping, laughing, and dancing. Everyone seemed to be enjoying the nightlife downtown, including me. The consumption of alcohol increased the need for me to powder my nose.

I excused myself from my date pushing through the crowd of partygoers bursting through the bathroom door. I ignored everyone that was waiting in line bombarding my way into the large stall in the corner. I could hear the women that had been standing in line patiently complaining and cursing, but I didn't care. I rummaged through my purse, pulling out the coke as my mouth watered waiting for a taste.

I snorted a small bit up my nostril leaning backwards, allowing the drip to take effect. I took one more hit before rubbing the excess on my gums and exiting from the stall. I smiled at all the women giving me dirty looks through the mirror as I checked myself out.

I had to hand it to my parents. They'd made an amazingly beautiful daughter. I doubt there was anyone on earth that would dispute that. I was tall, blonde, with thick, pouty lips, naturally full double D breasts that somehow managed to stay perky, a small waist, long legs, and a small but tight little ass!

I applied another coat of lipstick before checking my nose for any residue.

"All clear," I said under my breath before heading back to enjoy partying with Lutz. My 6 inch heels pounded the pavement, one stride at a time sending a jiggling sensation throughout my entire body. The effects of the cocaine were presenting itself and the feeling of invincibility was overwhelming me. I thrived in moments like this. I felt like I could conquer the world. Given the right platform I most definitely would.

I dropped my head causing my hair to fall in front of me then snapped it back for that wild untamed look. It was like everything was moving in slow motion. Their smiles, the laughs, his hand rubbing against her arm, all of it sent a feeling I'd never experienced before through my body. I stood there not moving until Ryan looked up noticing me.

His eyes narrowed, and if I weren't mistaken his plan was to walk right past me. However, I couldn't have allowed that happen. Maybe it was my pride, but that was not how this scene was going to play out. Not tonight, at least. For the moment I didn't care about my date, the club, how hot I looked wearing the $5500.00 Emilio Pucci gown I was in. Ryan was being disrespectful!

I get it okay? I know I'd walked out of the relationship a long time ago. That didn't give him the right to go flaunting someone else around. I looked her up and down truth was she was nothing special. To be quite frank, I was offended. How could he have gone from this to that?

I intentionally blocked their path. "Well look at what we have here," I said tilting my head to the side with the fakest smile ever plastered across my face. Yeah I know that was the most unoriginal line I could've ever come up with, but I was grasping for something. Anything! I needed a lifeline okay!

"Tawny," Ryan said, attempting to bombard his way past me. He knew better than to believe that was going to happen. I did the dismissing.

"And who is this?" I asked, staring at his date. She reached her hand out introducing herself as if I really gave a damn who she was. I looked at her, rolled my eyes, and returned my attention back to Ryan. She was clearly as stupid as she was ugly. Where could she have possibly gotten the idea that I was making her acquaintance?

I couldn't hold in my anger. I went off on Ryan about taking another woman out the same day we'd broken up. In response he told me he didn't give a damn about how I felt about situation. We went back and forth for quite some time before things got really ugly. It would've been okay had his new little girlfriend just stayed in her place and allowed things to pan out.

"I'm sorry I really don't want to be in the middle of this," she stated, seeming dazed and confused. "Excuse me." She said, before trying to step past me.

You see I don't understand why she had to invade my space. Her shoulder brushed against mine and one thing led to another, next thing I know I was clawing at her eyes and trying to pull her hair from the roots. To my surprise, she started to send blows my way. Her fists were clenched tightly as one hit after another pounded into my face catching me off guard.

I had to think fast. I used my height and weight to my advantage overpowering and slinging her to the ground. All I could think about was ground and pound, as I mounted her exchanging my own tight fisted blows. Next thing I know, I was being pulled up by security and removed from the club.

I remained calm as I was carried out of the club. Once security got me outside I realized I'd fucked up. I was on a damn date, not having a girls night out. I started to plead my case with the big man who stood blocking the door. I used every tactic I could to break him down. My sex appeal was the last resort and thank God it was enough to sway him in my direction and back into the club. Not before he threatened to ban me if I started anymore shit after being let back in. I promised him I wouldn't.

Relieved that I hadn't messed up my date with Lutz and praying he hadn't seen me getting dragged through the crowd, I thanked the bouncer with a kiss on the cheek. When I walked back up to the bar Lutz wasn't anywhere to be found. I looked around trying to get a glimpse of him. After about 20 minutes, I found him alright.

He was on the dance floor partying like he didn't have a care in the world. I stood at the bar still fuming from the fight I'd gotten into and the fact that my client had left me hanging. I ordered two more shots of vodka, on his tab!

I caught a glimpse of myself in the mirror, my hair had managed to get the wild sexy look I was hoping for but my lip was busted. It was swollen and slit on the upper right side. I cursed under my breath before asking for some ice. The bartender obliged handing over a small plastic cup. I slammed a few cubes into a napkin and held it up to my lip. The night turned out to be a disaster and all I wanted to do was get my money and go the hell home.

Lutz came back rocking and snapping his fingers off beat. He looked me in my eyes not even noticing my mood had changed and did some number where he went down to the floor and back up gyrating his entire body. Had this been a regular night I would've rolled my eyes and told him to get lost. But, I was on a date so I had to act civilized.

I smiled as I pretended to enjoy myself while hiding the busted lip behind the ice filled napkin. When my shots came I quickly scooped them up slamming one back after the other.

"Come on Claudia, let's dance," Lutz demanded, blowing his stinking breath in my face. I was more than annoyed. The more the night went on, the less attractive he became. By the time we headed back to his hotel room, I was spent and just ready to get the date over with.

"Take off your clothes," he demanded, when we reached the room. I convinced him to let me shower first. He agreed after some coaching, but none the less I was able to have my way. I sashayed into the bathroom, locking it behind me. I let out a low sigh examining my face in the mirror. Thank God the swelling had gone down and, other than a few scratches you couldn't even tell I'd been in a fight.

I hopped in the shower taking as long as I could before making my way back to Lutz. To be honest, I was praying his drunk ass was asleep by the time I got out so I could slide into the bed and collect the rest of my money in the morning. As luck would have it, he was wide awake even after the extended stay in the shower.

I stopped in mid stride noticing a third person in the room. I looked at Lutz with questioning eyes, but he only shrugged his shoulders nonchalantly. Neither man chose to say anything putting me on high alert. That cocaine buzz had been long gone and I was paranoid as hell. This was not a part of the plan.

I looked over at my bag, wishing that I'd taken it in the bathroom with me.

That way I could've excused myself secretly went back in and called Victor. No chance in that. I didn't want to seem suspicious or get these guys agitated. I mean after all Victor did say that this Lutz guy was a very good friend of his.

"Take off your shoes," the man standing by the door instructed. I looked at my client who nodded his head in agreement so I did as I was told.

"You shouldn't be looking at him, Claudia." The other man said. "I am the man who's going to pay you." He added pulling an envelope from the breast of his coat pocket. I chose not to give him any back talk.

"I thank you very much for your generosity Mr.?" I smiled pretending to be comfortable with the two men.

"My name is not important," he said sighing heavily. "I just need you to," instead of him finishing his sentence he placed his index finger up to his lips as if to quiet me.

As if on cue Lutz pushed me onto the bed violently. I wanted to scream, but I didn't, I couldn't, I was truly in fear for my life. I lay on the bed unable to move as Lutz sat on top of me, tying my arms and feet to the posts of the bed. I'd never been tied up before and under these circumstances the experience was undesirable. I didn't know if I should say something or remain quiet like I'd been instructed. I opted to do the latter.

"I hear you offer the ultimate girlfriend experience," the man at the door said smiling. I nodded my head. "Good girl." he hummed, seemingly pleased.

"Bondage is extra," I blurted out before I knew it. That happened sometimes. Sometimes my mouth did exactly what my brain told it not to do. That's how I'd gotten myself into trouble the majority of the time.

The man raised an eyebrow, motioning for Lutz to come. He whispered something in his ear before he disappeared into another part of the room. My heart pounded hard anticipating a response. I was unsure of who I was dealing with or what Victor had told them I was willing to do.

"Yes," he responded after eyeing me uncomfortably. "That is what Victor has told me. I have all of your money here, would you like for me to count it out for you?" he threatened more than asked. I shook my head no, pissed off that Victor hadn't mentioned any of this bullshit to me. I knew I should've turned this down the minute he'd stopped following protocol by having this guy come to my house.

My heart almost stopped when Lutz came in with a heavy duffle bag and began to pull all kinds of weird, scary, shit out of it. I knew they didn't think they were going to use any of that shit on me. I hadn't signed up for this. I was scared to death. This was the first time I'd ever been afraid on a date.

"Are you ok?" Lutz asked. "You look a little pale." He stated turning to his partner with a little smile on his face. I looked between the two men as their eyes spoke to one another a language I couldn't comprehend. I needed to get out of there quick. I started to panic twisting my arms

28

telling them to untie me. All of my words rained down on two pairs of deaf ears. They weren't listening to a damn thing I was saying. I finally found my voice and began to scream. Lutz stuffed a cloth into my mouth muffling the sounds that seemed to be belting from the bellows of my soul.

"Calm her down," the man said nonchalantly. Lutz pulled out a needle preparing to inject me. With what, I didn't fucking know. I tried to calm myself, I wanted them to see that despite my heavy breathing I was no longer a problem for them, but they weren't convinced. He jammed the needle into my arm unexpectedly as I watched the liquid disappear from the needle into my blood stream.

A single tear fell from my eyes before everything was black. I was out. No dream, or thoughts, just darkness.

CHAPTER THREE

The ride home in the limo was quiet. I couldn't remember anything that happened after me being tied to the bed. I woke up with my money lying on the dresser and my arms and feet untied. My body was sore as hell. I looked like I should've been cast in a horror movie.

Victor was at my house cooking breakfast when I arrived. He yelled for me to come into the kitchen, but I bypassed him and the food heading directly towards the bedroom. I didn't want to see him at all. I didn't know what to think. I wasn't sure how to feel.

I turned on the bath water sitting inside as the water ran. The steam was suffocating. The hot liquid hitting against my skin caused it to become red. It was a painful pleasure that I needed in the moment. The very first moment I'd ever felt dirty after an encounter. The very first time I left a date confused.

As the water rose I closed my eyes, allowing it to sting my wounds. There were cigarette burns, bruises, cut marks, and welts all over my body. I tried to lie back but it was too painful. I was so lost in my thoughts I didn't hear Victor walk into the bathroom until he said *oh my God*. He walked over to me touching one of my wounds causing me to flinch.

"What happened to you?" he asked seemingly concerned. I looked up at him as if to say, *you know what happened.* I didn't have the energy to argue with him. I continued dipping my sponge in the water then squeezing it over my body.

He continued to rant and rave about what they'd done to me never once suggesting we call the police. Never once picking up his phone to call them and threaten their lives. That wasn't an option. We didn't want the almighty Victor

Chastain being involved in anything like this. What would something like this do to his career? I rolled my eyes still not saying a word.

"Well say something, Tawny!" he demanded, through eyes that told me more than his mouth wanted to say. I chose to remain quiet. There wasn't anything for me to say. If these were his friends he knew what they were capable of and what their intentions were with me. He'd already managed to negotiate the price that I'd paid. He wouldn't let up. He was interrupting my peace of mind. I did the only thing I knew to do.

"Your 40% is in the pink envelop on the dresser," I responded never looking up at him. He rushed out of the bathroom towards the dresser. I could hear him sorting through the bills as he yelled out how he'd never send me out on another call with them again.

I wasn't concerned with going on another call, ever! I needed to get better. So it didn't matter who he wanted to send me on a date with, I wasn't fucking going.

I wasn't even going to be available for at least a month.

Considering, I wasn't going to be able to work looking the way I did, I was unsure as to how he thought he was doing me any favors. To be perfectly honest, everything he was saying to me sounded like a bunch of bullshit. I couldn't believe that I'd put up with him and his shit for so long. I knew he was a shady character, but never would I have believed he'd screw me like he had.

I was aware of the way he treated the others. Until that moment I'd believed that I was someone special to him. He'd watched me grow up. Hell he was even at the hospital celebrating my birth with my mother and father.

My dad! We were supposed to have lunch that afternoon. I was going to have to reschedule. I got out of the water being careful about drying off and slid into a silk nightgown. Victor was still going on and on about absolutely nothing. At least nothing I was going to listen to. I was rethinking our entire relationship. It wasn't going to work, not on a personal or business level.

"I need to call my dad," I said exasperated. I pulled out my phone asking Galaxy to call, "dad".

"Tawny, how's my baby girl doing?" he sang clearly happy to be hearing from me. I hated to tell daddy, I couldn't meet with him but he would've lost his mind if he saw me like this. Then I'd have to muster up a lie. He'd make me file a police report and things would just get overly complicated.

"I'm not feeling well today daddy," I stated, holding back tears. "I have a massive headache. So we're going to need to reschedule our lunch."

"Do you need anything darling?" he asked sounding concerned. I assured him I was fine and that I planned on getting some rest and we ended our call. Although I wasn't lying to him, I hated not being completely honest. I was his youngest child and his pride and joy. I never wanted to disappoint him. He'd always had high hopes for me. He believed in me and loved me when I felt like no one else had. For that I always wanted to protect him. It was natural for me to want to give him what he'd given me in return, happiness and peace.

Victor stood there staring at me as if he was waiting for something. I rolled over in my bed closing my eyes. Despite the pain of the beating I'd taken, I was able to fall asleep right away.

I was awakened from my sleep, by a loud crashing sound that came from downstairs. It was pitch black other than the moonlight that eerily illuminated my bedroom. I called out for Victor, he didn't answer. I reached for my phone that was usually on my nightstand, but it was gone.

I stood there next to my bed for what seemed like an eternity holding my breath, trying to figure out if I should move forward or stay put. I strained my eyes trying to locate my cell phone one more time, to no avail. I'd been meaning to get a gun, but hadn't gotten around to it yet.

I picked up the first thing I could find, which was a pair of dull ass scissors. I tiptoed through my condo listening for any movement. There was nothing. Then I heard voices. They were German voices, the same voices I'd heard the night before. My heart fell to my stomach as I tried to catch my breath. My entire body trembled despite me attempting to calm myself down.

Nothing was working. I remained paralyzed, not sure if I should lock myself in my bedroom or just stay put and stand my ground. Whatever, I decided I'd better hurry up because the voices were getting closer. I knew giving those men my address was a bad idea. I cursed Victor and as my anger was replaced with fear I made my move opting to lock myself in the bedroom.

Moments later I could hear rattling at the door. Someone was trying to get in. The two German men burst through the door just as I slid my body underneath the bed. I held my breath squeezing my eyes shut, hoping they didn't find me.

They were whispering to one another in their language. Dammit why had I only learned Russian, Spanish, and French? The anticipation was killing me and before I could stop myself the tears started to flow and a whimper escaped from my mouth.

Their shoes hit my hardwood floors with ground shaking thuds. Or at least that's what it felt like in that moment. I could hear my phone vibrating as the light flickered on and off. It must've been in my bed the entire time. I prayed silently hoping I got out of my room alive.

My mind ran a thousand miles per minute. Next, I found myself being dragged from beneath the bed by my feet. I kicked and screamed, trying to fight my way back to safety. Then I woke up! I looked around the dark room, my chest rising up and down causing pain to shoot through my entire body.

I was safe. I was at home, in my own bed.... SAFE! It was only a dream. A horrible nightmare, but my body let me know that the previous night was all too real. I rummaged through my covers picking up the cell phone that had saved me from my dream. It was Ryan.

At first I wasn't going to answer, but then I asked myself why not? He was a good distraction for the time being. Truth was Ryan was always a good distraction. Other than my dad, he was the only thing in my life that made sense at the moment. It was funny how it took something traumatic to happen for me to realize that. I answered the phone trying to sound "normal".

"Tawny, we really need to talk. Now!" Ryan demanded, catching me off guard. He'd never spoken to me like that. He was always gentle. Maybe I'd pushed him too far, walking out on him, and starting fights was something he wasn't used to.

I wanted to be around him right then. I was all alone and feeling like a prisoner in my own home. But, I couldn't. He'd surely go to my father and tell him that I'd been hurt. Not that it was a bad thing for my father to know, but it was a bad thing for me to have to explain why. I'd yet to figure out any lies to tell at the moment. And the way my head felt, I couldn't conjure up a lie even if I wanted to.

"I can't right now," I responded, although I didn't want to be alone.

"Well, I'm outside and you need to come open the door," he said. I knew if he'd taken the time to drive over he was not going to leave until he saw me. I pulled myself out of bed, maneuvering through the apartment to unlock the door.

"It's unlocked," I sighed before ending the call. I could hear Ryan fumbling around making his way to my bedroom.

Upon entering the room he flicked on the lights. I asked him softly to turn them back off. He did as he was told. I was thankful he hadn't seen what had become of my face. My eyes were swollen, my lip was busted, I looked horrid to say the least.

"Hey, are you alright?" he inquired sitting down on the bed lightly touching my hair. All I could do was break down crying. I'd held it in all day. I'm not sure how, but I assume the sleep helped a whole lot. When Ryan tried to hold me in an attempt to calm me down, I let out a painful yelp.

He immediately jumped up turning on the light. The sight of me caused him to rub his hands through his hair, then down his face. He sighed heavily, as I sat there waiting for his reaction. I couldn't bring myself to even look at him. I'm not sure if I was embarrassed or what. I just hated the way I looked. I hated what happened to me.

"Who did this to you?" he asked, as his nose flared and his eyes pierced through me causing me to become nervous. I wouldn't dare tell him the truth about what happened. I decided to just keep quiet. Maybe my silence would calm him down. He was always a pretty mild mannered fellow. Not that night. He questioned me again, this time bringing the volume up in his voice.

"I... I... I don't know," I stammered.

He paced back and forth as I begged him to relax. Even in taking a seat his jaw remained clenched tightly. He asked again who'd hurt me. Again I lied.

"Was it that guy you were with last night?" he asked. He just wouldn't let it go. Now I was starting to regret even letting him come in. For all this I could've stayed locked in my room having nightmares all night.

"What guy?" I asked playing dumb. That only seemed to infuriate him even more. He went on a rampage professing his love for me, then telling me he hated the fact that he cared so much. He didn't know why he'd put up with my shit for so long. Then he was comforting me. I had officially made Ryan lose his mind. Well at least temporarily.

I'd never seen him like that and I didn't like it one bit. What was even worse was I felt bad for being the cause of his confusion. He pulled his cell phone out to call my dad. Despite the pain that riddled my body, I hopped up snatching it from his hands.

"What the hell are you doing?" he spat.

I stared at him unsure of what to say. I felt like I needed a line. When things got too stressful the coke always calmed me down. It made me not care.

"I need to call your dad and you need to go to the police," he said this time more calm.

I continued to stare at him with pleading eyes still having not figured out what to say. He reached for his phone but I snatched it away.

"I can't!" I yelled. "Okay are you happy now?" I asked trying to manipulate the situation.

"Not today Tawny," he responded. "You won't make me feel bad about being the Good Guy." He said looking me directly in my eyes. His glare was so intense I had to look away. I didn't want him to notice what was hiding behind my eyes. I felt insecure for the first time. I wasn't sure of anything.

"Okay," I said, putting my hands up in the air in defeat. I begged him not to tell daddy, promising I'd tell him on my own time. In the meantime, I just needed him to be there with me. I was afraid. He told me I needed to go to the police, but I wasn't having it. What was I going to tell them? Two men had assaulted me and then paid me for a date my boyfriend/pimp had set up?

Speaking of which, where was he at anyway? Ryan wasn't supposed to be there consoling me. He was! It was his fault all of this was happening to me to begin with. As usual when things got sticky he disappeared. Considering the magnitude of what had gone down however, I would've never guessed he'd be missing in action. I guess that's what I got for guessing.

Ryan was satisfied with the story I was giving him and left it well enough alone after a few minutes. He lay behind me spooning me as he snuggled his head into my neck. I exhaled and was back off to sleep before even having the chance to talk to him about his little girlfriend. Oh well, we'd get to her later. For the time being I was just thankful to have him there.

CHAPTER FOUR

Two weeks had passed before I was able to cover my wounds with concealer and get out and about. I'd yet to hear from Victor but I knew he was just fine. He'd been present with some young brunette at one of my father's luncheons. That pissed me off. The bastard hadn't even called to check on me. Not until we ran into each other at my father's house.

"Hey Tawny, how've you been?" Victor asked, pretending as if he didn't know. Then again he didn't. Being that he snuck out of the house while I was sleeping and had yet to check back in.

"Just fine," I responded not even attempting to hide the contempt I was feeling towards him. My father looked at me funny asking if I was ok. I responded, great, before taking a bite out of an apple I'd snatched from the fruit bowl on the counter. I forced a fake smile on my face and gave him a kiss before heading out the door.

"I'd like to see you more often young lady," daddy called after me. "I don't want to go two weeks without seeing you ever again." He added as I closed the door. What he didn't know was those two weeks of not seeing him were like hell to me too. Daddy and I were very close. Although, he had three other children, I knew I was his favorite. The other three were money hungry worthless pieces of trash if you ask me.

I drove to the Cantina down the street from my condo, I needed a drink. I slid into the parking space directly in front of the door, watching the patrons go in and out. I sat there for a moment, before deciding to invite a couple friends.

"Hey Lacey," I sang into the phone. Before I could get anything else out the chatterbox started chattering. She was the gossip queen. She didn't mean any harm by it, she just loved being in other people's business. She'd always say, *"It's not gossip if it's the truth."* That was her way of justifying putting everyone's business out there. I'd just laugh. She'd been that way since I'd met her in kindergarten and she wasn't changing anytime soon.

I rolled my eyes up inside my head and smiled as she went on and on about people I didn't care to hear anything about. She stopped herself in mid-sentence.

"Oh my gosh!" she practically yelled into the receiver. "Where have you been for the past couple weeks?"

I knew that was coming. As much as I'd loved to have confided in my best friend, I couldn't have that business floating all around town. I told her I was out of town for a couple weeks needed some "me time". She bought it.

"Where did you go? I mean, I know you said you needed, "me time" but you could've invited me. I mean you are my best friend." She said, doing what she always did. If I had really been going out of town and told her she would've invited herself. Had her petite little body and bags waiting on my doorstep ready to skip town.

"Not far, I just needed some quiet." I responded, not wanting to elaborate too much. Changing the subject before she started asking too many questions I invited her over to the Cantina. She didn't waste any time accepting.

"I'm going to call Chantelle as well. We'll ride together." She said doing exactly what I'd expected her to do. Lacey, Chantelle, and I had been best friends since we were five years old. Even when we'd have our overly emotional falling outs we always managed to come back together stronger than ever.

I loved those two more than I loved my own sister. Then again they were my sisters. We just didn't share the same blood ties. My father was father and their parents were mine. They were heaven sent when I was going through issues with dad's ex-wife. They helped our family tremendously. They even made sure that I was able to get to all of my counseling sessions when daddy's job got to be too demanding. They were the village that helped raise me.

I smiled telling Lacey I'd get us a seat. It was almost evening and I knew the happy hour crowd would come pouring in soon. The Cantina could get pretty crowded on Friday's. It was the wind down spot for those who worked hard all week and needed to play a little.

By the time my girls had made it to the restaurant I was halfway done with my margarita. The urge to excuse myself and enjoy my last bit of powder had presented itself, but I opted against it. I really needed to discuss something with my friends. Their undivided attention was required and I needed to sell them on this dream.

"Of all the places, Tawny, you chose here?" Chantelle looked around with her nose scrunched up in the air. I'd bet my last dollar, her parents kept caviar in her bottle as an infant. She didn't want to be seen anywhere other than a 5 star restaurant and wouldn't wear anything unless it came from Nieman Marcus or

Saks. I rolled my eyes pretending to be annoyed.

"Chantelle, where would you have had us then?" I probed just to get a nice little chuckle.

"Anywhere but here," she responded, picking up a spotted piece of silverware then placing it back on the table as if it were diseased. I motioned for the waitress to come over ordering three margaritas before I began speaking.

"So, what's been up ladies?" I asked, trying to break the ice before going in for the kill. I'd been going back and forth with this for the past two weeks and now was the time to present it.

"Same ol' same ol'," Chantelle responded, still looking "stuck up". "But what's been going on with you? I heard you had a fight," she said, staring at me hard and long.

I chuckled a bit thinking about the run in I'd had with Ryan's little date. Speaking of such, we'd yet to talk about her. I made a mental note to bring that up when I got home later. He had been at the house every night since the "incident", but with things the way they were I'd forgotten all about it.

"I wouldn't call it a fight," I responded, trying to downplay that entire situation. I didn't need anyone to know that Ryan and I had briefly broken up. Why did they have to know when we were back together?

Or at least that was how I felt until I seen Ryan pressing through the crowd with the brunette beauty on his arm. I wanted to get up and cause a scene, but I couldn't. Not in front of my friends. I pretended as if I hadn't seen them and hoped that the place got crowded enough that they didn't see them either.

"Tawny!" Lacey said, snatching me out of my thoughts.

"I'm sorry what did you say?" I responded shaking the image of Ryan and that... that... Bitch, out of my head.

"I said, what do you call it then?" Chantelle said, folding her arms leaning back in her chair.

I told them that was not what I invited them out for. I forced a smile across my face asking them if they were interested in a business opportunity. They exchanged glances with one another before placing their focus back on me. I knew my girlfriends loved money and hated working hard at anything.

I also knew that unlike me they were still enrolled in school. As a matter of fact they were enrolled in two different universities. That meant one very important thing. They had access to the girls. Lots of beautiful college girls who were broke and needed cash. Not only did they need money, but they didn't have a whole lot of time on their hands to make the kind of money that allotted them to live the lifestyle every young girl should live. Fast money was a good way to get what they wanted while getting an education.

"So, you ladies have been wondering where I've been," I smiled stating the facts.

Chantelle looked impatient while Lacey was of course hanging onto every word that came out of my mouth.

I made up this cockamamie story about how I'd run into a woman while vacationing who was "dating". Upon talking to her I was overcome by this realization. I waited for them to respond to what I'd said. Chantelle took the bait.

"So what she was on a date. Why in the hell does her dating give you realization?" she huffed impatiently.

I rolled my eyes at her sarcasm, before continuing glad that Lacey was there to even out the tension. That girl had an attitude for days.

"When, I say date, I mean a paid date," I said still beating around the bush. Chantelle caught on, but Lacey looked confused as hell.

"Okay so you met a hooker," Chantelle interrupted seeming less than amused and not the least bit entertained.

"Wait hold up," Lacey said, taking a sip of her Margarita and throwing her hands in the air. "Where did you get hooker from that?" I loved my friend dearly, but she had zero common sense. However, there was rhyme and reason for involving her in this little scheme of mine. She had the gift of gab. She talked so fast even I couldn't keep up with her sometimes. That was great for marketing and even greater for recruitment.

Chantelle rolled her eyes before explaining what she thought was, "the business". Chantelle sat back with a satisfied look on her face before taking a large gulp of her drink. She was so sure she'd had the business down to a T. Unfortunately she didn't.

"Anyway," I said looking at Chantelle then back and Lacey. "I was thinking why don't we start our own escort service?" I blurted out. I was tipsy and I couldn't hold it in any longer. I didn't want to work for or with Victor anymore. I was money to him nothing more, nothing less. And if I was going to be risking my life for anyone it would be for me, myself, and I.

"Are you fucking crazy?" Chantelle asked, raising her voice up a level. I knew that was coming. Every time we'd decided to do something crazy and off the wall she was always the one I'd have to do the most convincing with.

"Chantelle," I started, before leaning closer towards her. "Think about how much money you'd make. I wrote some numbers on a napkin and slid it over to her. We'll get 40% of that." I smiled.

She didn't look impressed. She argued that considering we'd be splitting it 3 ways it wasn't enough money for the headache.

"Not only that, how in the hell do we know how to be pimps anyway?" she asked. "What are we going to do if these bitches don't give us our money?" she huffed. "I can't fight, you can't fight, and Lacey damn sure isn't going to be busting any grapes in anyone's backyard in the near future." She spat. I chuckled at the thought of us coming up to someone talking about *Bitch better have my money.*

"You're worried about the wrong thing," I said. "They're going to pay us our money and if they don't we'll end their contract."

"Look," Chantelle said, getting up from her seat. "I have parents who make sure I have everything I need. I'm not following behind you and another one of your schemes." She stated before walking towards the door.

Lacey and I watched her walk out the door. It always went one of two ways. Lacey was either with me or she didn't choose a side. So with her not running behind her ride I knew she was in. I smiled asking her if she was ready to make some money. She giggled nodding her head. I held up my fist waiting for her to smack hers against mine. Almost simultaneously our attention moved towards the couple that was making their way past us hand in hand.

Ryan looked right at me without saying a word. And that little "girlfriend" of his had the nerve to look down on me too with a smirk on her face. As pissed as I was I didn't make a move. Not because Lacey had grabbed hold of my arm, but because I couldn't. I needed to save face.

Before, I had no control over my actions, but in that moment I refused to react. After spending two whole weeks nursing me back to health he decided to do this. I was under the impression we'd made up. We had slept with each other on numerous occasions while he was at my house.

I pulled out my phone, sending a brief text. *I guess you don't love me as much as you said you did.* I turned off my phone, before signaling for the waitress to bring us another round. I pushed Ryan and his shenanigans to the back of my mind. I would deal with him later. For the time being, I had to give Lacey a quick rundown of the business.

"And this girl," she said completely infatuated with the idea of us becoming "madams". "She gave you all of this information, just like that?" she asked.

"Yeah," I responded. "It was like she needed someone to talk to. You know, get some things off her chest," I lied. Lacey bought into every single detail.

"What about a name?" I asked, still not clear on what to call ourselves. Everyone had names like Elite, Premiere, etc. I couldn't think of anything.

"You said she provided all services right?" Lacey asked. I nodded my head. "They call these full service dates the Girlfriend Experience correct?" she asked. Again I nodded. "Why not call it that?"

"What?" I asked, not sure I was following her.

"The Girlfriend Experience!" she smiled. As dingy as she was for some reason the name worked for me. It was simple and to the point.

Providing a man or woman with the ultimate erotic experience was the plan. It was our only goal. Our clients had to feel like what they were getting was an experience unlike any other. My mind started churning. I told Lacey before we started recruiting I needed to learn the business firsthand just so I'd know how to train our girls.

She looked at me like I was crazy, but eventually I got her to cave into the idea that I would be sleeping with men for money. She would market my services, serving as my own personal assistant. I suggested that she start that night.

"Right here in the Cantina?" she asked.

"No better time than the present." I smiled. With that Lacey began to work her magic. I sat back satisfied although I wasn't out the woods yet, I was seeing the light clear out the darkness of the tunnel.

CHAPTER FIVE

Five weeks of working for myself and business was booming. I couldn't have done a better job myself. Lacey had me busy as hell. It helped that I'd taken a few regulars along with me. I was thriving. I decided who I went on dates with and when. We did extensive background, and reference checks to ensure safety. To get the girlfriend experience you'd have to be more than just a paying customer, you'd have to be a good one.

We were finally in the recruiting stages and unlike any other escort service around we had training classes. I know what you're thinking how in the hell could we have training classes? Well, I'd teach the girls how to properly perform in their line of duty. There were certain tricks of the trade that kept our customers hooked.

Other than looking great our ladies had to be in good health. We checked monthly for STD's and any other problems that may cause them to be unable to perform. We conducted tests to determine a girls' stress level. If they were too high she was no longer a candidate.

The ladies of GFE Incorporated had to adhere to a specific diet to maintain a healthy weight. We hired a Registered Dietician to put together meal plans. We even provided gym memberships for the first three months to make sure the girls stayed tight and right.

We were still looking into getting a deal on hip baths. They were supposed to keep the vagina tight and free of unwanted bacteria. We were running GFE like a true incorporation. All of our paperwork was in order and we would be paying taxes regularly. The IRS didn't care where their money came from, as long as they got it. I wanted to keep them off of our backs as much as possible.

Each of our girls was an independent contractor. We were the "middle man" so to speak and not their employer. Being part of our organization was merely a good business investment for them individually. We charged top rates for our services so our girls never felt cheated out of paying us the finder's fee.

Training class was a little more challenging than I had anticipated, but I was happy that Lacey could handle difficult people. There was one girl in particular who worked my last nerve. Ms. Amanda swore she knew it all. If someone had an experience she had that same experience except ten times more interesting than her peers. She knew the business all too well, but had not one day of damn experience. I guess she read a lot.

"So, you work for us, and yet you get 40% of the money we make doing all the work?" she questioned as I went over the pay scale for the company.

Lacey could sense my frustration with this little red headed bitch so she took over.

"Well, Amanda," she started breaking everything down. "We need that 40% for several different things other than just income for our pockets." she started, before Chantelle came bursting through the door.

"Nothing's wrong with asking questions, but let's be clear Ms.?" Chantelle started, seemingly unfazed by Amanda and her line of questioning. Lacey started to tell her what her name was but Chantelle cut her off in typical diva style. "You know what it doesn't even matter. The fact remains that we're taking the bulk of the risk. If you get arrested for being... STUPID! Then we have to come bail you out. We pay for your monthly testing being if you decide to be stupid again and have unprotected sex. That isn't cheap you know? Then you're getting free marketing with our good name and brand supporting you. We provide your business cards. We pay for background checks. We call references."

Chantelle could've went on and on but I decided that Ms. Amanda had heard enough. I watched her face turn beet red in embarrassment as Chantelle gave her a dose of what she'd been trying to dish out to Lacey and I.

"With that being said," I interrupted. "You're still in control and have the option to opt out at any given time. There's the door." I motioned with my hands giving anyone the opportunity to leave.

"Great, then everyone is on board," Chantelle said sarcastically. "Now, we can move forward."

Chantelle went on to explain that we were not in the business of prostitution. Any money received for any sexual favors were clearly between the individual girl and the client. The client's money was merely a "donation" for her TIME. We went through all the shenanigans of covering our asses and our girls' asses so we stayed out of jail.

When day 1 of training was over I was exhausted. My work was never done. I had to make my way to see a client later that night. The plan was we'd have a late dinner a nice little "recap" and then I could go home and get in my bed. Before, all of that I needed to speak to Chantelle.

After the last girl left the office space we'd rented I was all over it. "I thought you were out," I said, walking up behind her.

She didn't miss a beat. "Well now I'm in," she said nonchalantly taking a sip of the wine Lacey had just popped open in celebration of a successful first day.

I looked her up and down waiting for more but she wasn't biting. She wasn't getting off that easily. Not after she'd stormed out of the Cantina as if my idea beneath her.

"You changed your mind, huh?" I huffed, still almost breathing down her neck. That must've been rubbing her the wrong way because next thing I knew she'd snapped her neck around and was staring me up and down. I swear Chantelle was everything any of us ever believed about a black woman. Sexy, sassy, with an attitude not many could handle.

"Listen, don't keep asking me all these questions Tawny," she said, as if I was just going to stop probing.

"Then tell the truth," I responded sarcastically.

"Daddy's cutting me off," she sighed heavily.

That was the truth that I surely didn't want to hear. Let alone as to why he was cutting his precious little Chantelle off. She was his pride and joy. There was nothing that she asked for that she didn't get. She didn't have to beg or explain why she wanted it. If she said that she wanted to take a trip to the moon and there was a spaceship headed up there she'd be on it.

"I don't know what to say," was all I could muster.

"Well then don't say anything," she snapped at me. I knew she was pissed so I wasn't upset that she was less friendly than usual. In her own time she would tell me what was going on. I guess now just wasn't the time nor the place to discuss it.

"So," Chantelle started. "If I were to go on a few dates... You know, just to learn the business firsthand would I be able to keep 100% of my profit?" she asked.

The thing was what applied to the others didn't apply to us. We could work however, we wanted. If she wanted 100% then she'd get it.

"Chantelle," Lacey said, appalled by what our friend was considering doing. "You're really going to do this?" she asked as if it was something unbelievable. I almost felt offended by the way Lacey made it sound. She never questioned me about doing it. Why try to talk Chantelle out of it?

Lacey saw how I looked at her and attempted to save face. "What?" she said acting like her line of questioning was appropriate. "Everyone knows you like to fuck Tawny." She added, as if to say *duh.*

We burst into laughter. Lacey was telling the truth. If no one knew anything else about me they could count on that fact that. I was called every kind of whore in the book since I was twelve years old. It started when Richey Moore told everyone in the school that I sucked his itty bitty dick. The crazy part about it was that he was telling a damn lie. My mouth never went anywhere towards his little penis. He was just upset that I told him it was small.

And it was small, a lot smaller than I'd seen on daddy's porn. I wasn't going to lie. Instead of denying to have done such a thing, I decided to play along and tell everyone how little he was and how fast he came. As if we knew anything about size or coming. I mean his balls hadn't even dropped yet. I chuckled a little longer at that thought. We were some crazy kids.

"She got you there," Chantelle said, shoulder bumping me, causing me to spill a bit of wine over my fingers. I sat my glass down to wipe off my hands when my phone started ringing.

It was Ryan. He'd left several messages since the night at the Cantina. He'd even showed up to my place, but I didn't have anything to say. Really? He thought it was okay to just prance around town with this girl after she put her hands on me? Okay, so what I put my hands on her first, but she got the best of me so that didn't count. She won I lost which meant I got to keep the guy all to myself. The same guy I'd been with practically half of my existence on earth.

I hit reject while my two best friends stared at me. There was an awkward silence that was making me way too uncomfortable.

"What?" I yelled, before slamming back my wine.

"Do you want to talk about it?" Lacey asked rubbing my back gently.

"Oh my God, Lacey, I'm not a damn puppy!" I said, moving away from her hand. "Plus there's nothing to talk about." I shrugged my shoulders pretending as if I didn't care.

Here's my moment of truth, but don't get too used to these, I did care. No this wasn't my pride talking or me being the spoiled brat that I've been known to be. Ryan had genuinely hurt my feelings. I mean, sure I had fucked up big time. I got it. Everyone is entitled to a fuck up. Right?

You just don't go moving on to someone else flaunting them around town unless of course you were already on to them to begin with. As far as I was concerned Ryan and Victor were both no more. Yes Victor had been trying to get in touch with me as well. After he'd totally disappeared on me as if I was just business as usual, I was finished.

There wasn't one damn thing we needed to talk about as far as I was concerned. If anything he could've given me his percentage of cash that got me drugged, beaten, and tortured for hours. But, that was neither here nor there, I was just happy to be alive.

I shook my head, trying to rid myself of the few memories I did have of that night. The nightmares were still plaguing me, but what could I do other than move on? Nothing. So that was exactly what I was doing, looking straight forward and not dwelling on the past.

"Alright, Chantelle," I started, as the three of us began to clean the office space together. "I think I have the perfect role for you to play." I said as the wheels in my head began to churn idea after idea.

"Based on your possessive and aggressive personality you'd be the perfect Dominatrix. How about we call you Temptress X-Crucia?" I suggested thinking about how painful it would be to have her as a girlfriend. Lacey chuckled, causing Chantelle to shoot her a nasty look. I held in my laugh. I mean the name fit her so well. She was a beautifully tempting pain in the ass, nuts, brain, and whatever else required tenderness to the touch.

"I was thinking more like Lady Heroine," she responded seriously. I couldn't hold it in any longer and neither could Lacey. We both burst out laughing. "What's so funny?" Chantelle asked without cracking a smile.

It was obvious what was so funny. The name was not very sensual or erotic, unless you were a heroin addict or enjoyed getting your rocks off shooting meth or something.

71

"Ok, ok," I said holding my hands up in retreat. Maybe we just needed to hear her out. I wasn't sold on the name and we ALL needed to be sold on the name. "What's the logic behind this Lady Heroin name?"

"Of course you two wouldn't get," she spat sarcastically.

"Well explain it," I challenged her waiting to hear how that shit panned out.

"Lady is self-explanatory. I have always been such. I mean look at me, everything about me screams elegance and feminism. Heroin because I'm dope." she responded.

Now that was a word I'd never heard her use before. Who in the hell was she hanging with that had her speaking, slang, ebonics, or whatever it's called? Lacey and I exchanged glances.

"Dope?" Lacey laughed.

Chantelle didn't seem the least bit amused. In all honesty for some odd reason she'd taken offense to Lacey questioning her vernacular.

"Yes, dope," Chantelle said copping more attitude than usual. "I want to have that effect."

"What effect?" Lacey asked.

"When they are with me they can be everything they wish they were. I can make them feel that way. I can make them feel loved and at peace like nothing or no one else matters in the world except them. Keep them warm and cozy. Then when it's time for them to come down, I can be that violent pain." She said as if it was nothing.

Lacey and I stared at her as she continued putting files away in the drawer. She stopped and asked if we were going to put up a website for GFE as if she hadn't totally went almost psycho serial killer in her description on us.

"Well we wanted to be as discreet as possible," Lacey responded, sounding unsure of if she'd really wanted to say anything at all.

"Why would we not do that when we need to get our name out there?" she asked. "I was doing some research and there's this company around here called Signature Elite." The sound of them made me cringe on the inside but I kept my game face on.

"What about them?" I inquired, seeing where she was going with all this.

"Well they've been around for years and are our only competition," she responded. "The way I see it, if we are going to do this we need to monopolize. Now I went to their website and saw the best that they had to offer and those girls have nothing on ours." She stated having a point.

She'd even gone as far as to call in for general information, although she said the owner "Vic" wasn't too keen on speaking about business over the phone. She said she decided to go meet up with him to "infiltrate" his system. She used that exact word "infiltrate". She never ended up meeting with him because Mr. Chastain had shown up at the restaurant so she had to go. She didn't need her dad any more upset with her than he already was. She was unaware that Vic was Mr. Chastain.

She was right we should've had a website. For the girls who were ok with showing their faces they could. For those who weren't we'd manage to hide them. It was a great thing Chantelle knew a photographer who had a small studio downtown. Things were coming together very well. Three heads were most definitely better than one.

CHAPTER SIX

"I couldn't believe that I was standing at that hotel room door about to do it, but I was. My heart was filled with anticipation and fear. I was ready to run and ready to go in and get it over with all at the same time.

The lump in my throat let me know that if I didn't get myself together quickly I'd be hurled over someone's feet by the time the door opened. I was actually surprised to see a woman standing before me urging me to come in. She was as elegant as I was although not as pretty.

She was tall and domineering and if I wasn't as secure as I am in myself I may have been intimidated. I smirked as I let myself in her room thinking ok it's now or never. She started to speak, but I put on my best sista girl accent and told her to shut up as I took in the entire room inch by inch. She didn't dare let out a sound, and that was how I liked it.

Those acting classes I'd hated taking as an elective in high school had really come in handy. I placed my briefcase on the table unlocking it with shaky hands. My entire body was jittery. Pulling out a pair of long black latex gloves I slid them up my arms, making a slapping sound upon completion. I then placed a small silk napkin on the table. I pulled out the items I'd packed one at a time, making sure I held them up just long enough for her to see.

Every now and then I'd glance over my shoulder to see her reaction. I then demanded her to take off her clothes never taking my eyes off of what I was doing. I positioned myself to where all she could see was my back as I arranged my tools.

"Open your legs and rub your clit." I instructed with my back still turned. I could hear her breathing becoming heavy behind *me. To my surprise, I was becoming aroused myself. I could feel my juices soaking my black satin panties.*

I turned around removing my jacket displaying my firm caramel breasts that were pushed almost to my chin by a shiny black corset that took my waist in about 2-3 inches. My nipples were barely covered by the slippery looking fabric. Their roundness poking out like two milk chocolate drops. My stomach was as flat as a washboard. My finely tone legs were covered just past the knee with black thigh high boots that had zippers on all four sides. My efforts in maintaining a soft but firm body had yet to fail me. My client looked me up and down lustfully.

"Hey!" I yelled demanded her full attention. "Look me in my eye's!" I explained to her she wasn't in control I was and she would be doing exactly what I said when I said it. She opened her mouth to speak, but I cut her off immediately. "You don't speak unless I tell you to." I said, giving her the look of death.

Things were starting to get fun. This was how I wanted to treat people on most days and now I was getting paid to do it. I directed her to stand up and turn around as I held a black paddle in my hand softly patting my palm. I didn't like pain, but I was damn sure into inflicting it on others.

"Bend over," I whispered firmly pushing her head down towards the cushion of the chair. I stood back looking at her in that position. Her slender legs were spread just enough for me to get a glimpse of the most pretty pussy I'd ever seen in my life.

Her lips were perfect and everything was pink. It glistened with moisture urging me to place my hands on her small round behind and give it a shake. Her hot spot released air as I separated her inside lips giving me a better glimpse of the pinkness that hid deep within.

She let out a whimper as her hips swayed from side to side anticipating what would come next. I took my index finger rubbing it over her clit then sliding it inside of her. She moaned tightening her muscles around my finger. I slide it in and out a few more times before removing my finger and rubbing my wet glove over her ass. The *traces of the wetness on her beige skin turned me on.*

Then without notice I pulled my paddle back smacking her on her ass. Her hands slipped off the sides of her chair. I directed her not to allow them to slip again. Her hands were gripping the sides of the chair so tightly I could see her knuckles becoming white. I smiled, feeling completely in control."

"It was actually fun!" Chantelle laughed. She was happier than I'd seen her in a long time. I was assuming the problems she was having with her dad were weighing in heavy on her. It was good that GFE Inc. was taking some of that stress off of her.

"I would've never thought that whoring would set me so... free!" she whispered, grinning from ear to ear. After putting it like that I couldn't do anything but laugh. I guess she was in the right business because our phones were ringing off the hook for Lady Heroin.

She was a whopping 5'4" inches tall and full of attitude. Let her tell it she'd had those customers screaming for mercy and more at the same damn time. She even described one call in great detail. Not that I wanted to hear all of them, but because she was my friend and she was happy I listened. She was hot so I didn't mind having the visual of her fucking someone's brains out either.

"Wow," managed to escape my mouth as I looked at Chantelle in awe. I'd never seen her that excited about anything.

"I know," Lacey added. "I was about to have an orgasm right here at the table." She added causing all of us to chuckle. I looked at both of my girls faces. Who would've ever guessed we'd be involved in this type of business? This definitely was not what our parents had planned for our lives. But, we were making great money. It was our own. We were maintaining a lifestyle similar to what they'd been able to provide for us all of our lives. All we had to do was be pretty.

Sure it came with its ups and downs. But for all of us the good outweighed the bad. We ran an airtight organization. There was no stone left unturned. We'd even recruited one of the law students Lacey went to college with to help us make sure we dotted all of our I's and crossed those T's. Things were running as smoothly as ever. The money? Well let's just say we were pushing old Vic out of the business.

The girls and I exchanged a few more laughs before parting ways. I was tired. I'd taken the day off to just relax. I was still having nightmares every night to the point where I was afraid to go to sleep. The dreams were so vivid that I couldn't decipher rather they were real or not. I was thinking about going to a therapist, but opted out of doing that. I just needed to give myself some time to sort through everything. I mean other than the obvious I wasn't even sure what had happened that night. It all could've very well been consensual.

I pulled up in my driveway in a daze. As I got out of my car I was greeted by Victor. He wasted no time pinning me up against the car asking me why I hadn't been returning any of his phone calls. I was completely caught off guard by his actions. I'd never seen him angry a day in my life. This was a new side of the man I once loved. However, I couldn't let him know that he'd move me one bit. So I pretended to be unfazed.

"Can you please move out of my way?" I asked, contorting my face. He stepped back a little, but not enough to let me pass by. My body stiffened as I asked him again, but to no avail.

"Who the fuck do you think you are Tawny?" he asked pointing at me. His finger was so close to my face it was almost touching my nose.

My heart hit my chest with a thud over and over as I tried to keep myself calm. I couldn't do anything but stare at him. No words would come out of my mouth. I realized I was standing there lips moving but nothing. He slammed his hand against the top of my car next to me causing me to flinch.

"Did you hear me ask you a question?" he seethed. I was not ok with how he was talking to me at all. I didn't know how to react.

"Vi-victor," I stuttered laying the palms of my hands softly on his chest. "What are you talking about?" I asked. That's when he went on and on about me stealing his clients. Telling me that he owned me and I owed him this and that.

Clearly he was out of his mind. He didn't own me. Sure he taught me a lot about the business and got me connected with a few good people but I'd done all the work. I was even assaulted because he lied to me about some sadist pricks. The more he rambled on about what I was doing to him the less afraid I became. That fear was turning into anger.

I attempted to brush past him, but he pushed me back hard against the car telling me that I wasn't going anywhere. He made it very clear that he was not done talking to me. Despite the fact that he was a man I was ready to fend for myself.

"As far as I'm concerned this conversation is over." I responded, standing upright staring him directly in his eyes.

"What did you just say to me?"

I wasn't about to repeat myself. He was really starting to get on my last nerve. Who in the hell did he think he was? I attempted to push him out of my way with my chest, but he pressed himself firmly against me overpowering me.

"Get the hell out of my way," I said, raising my voice as I pushed past him. My heels made an echo as they pounded against the pavement. Victor was on my heels, mumbling under his breath. I'd hoped he didn't think he was going to come into my home. He was not welcomed. I'd changed the locks for a reason.

I unlocked the door hurriedly and slid inside. His foot caught the door before it closed. He was trying to pry himself in. I threatened to call the police. He countered with how bad of an idea that would've been. However, I wasn't backing down. He had a hell of a lot more to lose than I did. I made sure he kept that at the forefront of his mind before trying to enter my apartment anymore.

He caught my drift and decided that now was not the time or place to handle the "situation." He'd even had the nerve to ask me if I was willing to sit down with him to discuss the "problem".

"Victor there is no problem," I responded before slamming the door in his face. I leaned my back against the door and allowed myself to exhale. My adrenaline was pumping. I thanked whatever and whoever had their eyes on me and got me inside my home safely.

I slid out of my heels as I made my way into the kitchen dropping my keys on the counter. I needed a glass of wine. I popped open a bottle thinking long and hard.

"I need a gun," I said a loud to no one in particular. Between those crazy ass Germans and now Victor shit was starting to get way out of hand.

My phone began to ring causing me to damn near jump out of my skin. I looked at the caller id not recognizing the number. I sighed debating on rather I should answer it or not. For all I knew there was more drama than I could handle on the other line. I opted not to pick up and commenced to sipping on my Moscato.

My phone started to ring again this time it was Lacey.

"Hey, chicka!" I smiled into the phone. Her calls were always welcomed and she was a good distraction from the nonsense that was plaguing my mind at the moment.

"Hey," she responded out of breath. Before I could ask her what was wrong, she dropped the bomb on me. She told me that she needed me to meet her down at the police station Amanda had been arrested.

"Arrested!" I exclaimed, feeling a rise in my temperature as the word resonated through my brain. Lacey didn't respond so I took that as my queue to continue. "Arrested, for what?" I said with my voice still raised.

"Just meet me down at the station," she responded.

Before I left out of the house I called Loretta our attorney telling her we needed her right away. She assured me she'd be there before I was before hanging up the line. My phone started ringing again from the same unknown number as before.

"Hello?" I said into the receiver clearly agitated. Whoever was on the other line better have hoped they were ringing my line for a good cause.

"Tawny, it's me," Amanda sobbed into the telephone. "I'm in jail." She wailed uncontrollably.

As much as that girl got on my last nerve I felt sorry for her. She knew nothing about this business but one thing she had to keep in mind at that moment was to keep her mouth shut. I spoke to her softly, causing her sobbing to calm down so she could clear her mind a bit and listen.

"Do not say a word," I instructed. "Not even during this phone call. Loretta is on her way." I added.

"Who's Loretta?" she asked sniffling.

"That's your attorney," I stated calmly walking out of my front door to my car. "You're going to be okay, I'm on my way also." I assured her. She acknowledged understanding we said our goodbyes and I sped down to the station. This was going to be a long ass night.

CHAPTER SEVEN

They kept Amanda detained all
weekend. They told us that she wouldn't
be released until she saw the judge,
Monday morning. I was up bright and
early to meet Loretta down at the
courthouse and show my support. I didn't
know what the hell was going on.

I remained Amanda's support
system not just for her benefit, but for
ours as well. One person could bring down
our entire organization and I refused to
allow that to happen. Not that we
promoted prostitution. In fact everything
that came out of our mouths and that was
drawn up on paper clearly prohibited it.
But, I wasn't a fool. Just how we were able
to slide through the cracks to do what we

did, there were overzealous worker bees looking to boost their careers by locking as many people up as they possible. Lying was a sure fire way to climb their way up the ladder.

I stood outside the courtroom talking to Loretta when Victor and a group of his buddies walked up. They were having a nice conversation laughing and carrying on as they stopped directly in front Judge Greggs courtroom. I squinted my eyes, not sure of rather I should say anything or keep quiet. I opted to remain silent.

When it was time we all walked into the courtroom together. Amanda's face was red and swollen by the time she entered the courtroom causing me to feel extreme grief for her. It looked like she'd been crying all weekend. Loretta fought for Amanda tooth and nail.

Victor had come up with so many bogus charges to get her "off the streets" so to speak it didn't make any sense. No one knew Mr. DEA Office was running the now second largest escort service in the state. They also didn't know he snorted more cocaine than a Colombian Drug Lord. I wanted to object to every damn word that came out of his mouth. He was abusing the system that was supposed to be used to protect and serve.

What he should've been concerned with was finding the bastards who had assaulted me. Maybe then he would still be monopolizing in the "industry". Just maybe he wouldn't be scrounging for a way to maintain his drug habit and lifestyle. I muttered inaudibly under my breath.

I sat there with my arms crossed and lips puckered tight. Every now and then Victor would glance back at me with this stupid smirk plastered across his face. All the sexiness I used to see in him was gone. However, I got the last laugh when the judge reamed him a new asshole about wasting her time after Loretta laid him out to dry.

Amanda sat there looking confused, but that was okay all she needed to know was that when everything was said and done she'd be going home. Nothing was going to be on her record. As we left the courtroom Victor smiled at me as we met at the doors to exit the room.

"Hey, there Tawny, and how are you doing sweetheart?" he asked going to hug me. I backed away, giving him a dirty look. He held his hands up high, looking from me to Amanda and then Loretta. "Oh, I'm sorry, is this your friend?" he asked, pretending to not know of our relationship.

I looked at him without answering. I wasn't there to play games, especially in the presence of Amanda and Loretta. "Well listen," he taunted patting me on my back. "Tell your father, I said hello and I look forward to seeing him on the golf course very soon." He grinned.

"Do you know that prick?" Loretta asked, watching him walk away, giving him the same shit face as I. I nodded my head not wanting to elaborate anymore on it.

"Amanda, I'm going to take you home, alright?" I said, trying to change the subject and get the hell away from the courthouse. She nodded her head in agreement as she followed me to my car. When she sat down in the BMW she burst out crying again. I wasn't sure what to do so I chose to pat her softly on the back, allowing her to let her tears flow.

"Oh my God Tawny, thank you so much for coming to get me!" she cried, clearly shaken up by what she'd just gone through. "I don't know if I'm cut out for this." She sobbed.

I wanted to tell her to shut the hell up she knew what she'd signed up for, but I couldn't. I wouldn't dare treat her like that. Truth was, this lifestyle wasn't for everyone. Sure, it was great when we were making money and having fun. But, just like with everything else when things got tough people folded.

I allowed her to rant and rave about how she'd wanted out. "Are you mad at me?" she asked, through red puffy eyes.

Hell yeah, I was mad, but I don't know if I was necessarily mad at her. I needed to know more about why she'd gotten arrested.

"What happened?" I asked, keeping my eyes on the road. I didn't want to look at her. My nose flared a bit and I could feel myself becoming hot. I was prepared for collateral damage in this business, but if things could be avoided they needed to be at all costs.

"I did everything like I normally do, like you guys taught me," she responded sincerely. "I never once agreed to have sex for money. After everything was said and done they burst through the doors and arrested me." Amanda responded, before breaking down in tears again. "They put me in handcuffs before I had any clothes on!"

I sat there pissed. What kind of shit was that? Was it even legal? I asked her if she told Loretta that. She said she had. That was most definitely a violation of her rights. What right did they have to bust into the room and arrest her for anyway? They did this after the fucking had already taken place. If this was a sting, then they should've been in there once the money and the verbal confirmation of what the money was for were established. I kept a mental note of what Amanda told me.

"Do you want a drink?" I asked. I'd been worried about her all weekend.

"I'm not old enough to drink," she responded, tilting her head to the side. I rolled my eyes.

"I know how old you are," I said. "Do you want a drink or not?"

"Yeah," she said. "I really don't want to be alone right now."

I burst a U-turn in the middle of the road and headed over to a little spot a client of mine owned. I looked over at Amanda thinking twice about taking her out. She looked horrible.

Against my better judgment, I moved forward as planned and before you know it, we found ourselves slamming shots and playing darts. She was having a great time. So great that she started to speak freely about a whole lot of things. For instance, I hadn't known that before I'd arrived at the courthouse Loretta was outside having an in depth conversation with Victor.

"They looked mighty cozy to me," Amanda slurred as she threw a dart damn near toppling over.

"Cozy?" I asked fishing for more information.

"Yea!" she stated. Leaning forward "They even kissed," she whispered.

"What?" I asked raising my voice.

I played it cool even though I was seething on the inside. Why had she been acting as if she couldn't stand Victor in my presence? Furthermore, if they had something going on what good would she be as our attorney? I was going to find out the extent of their relationship. Depending on how that turned out she just might lose a client.

I was fully aware that lawyers were a lot like doctors. It didn't matter what side of the fence they were on they typically ran in the same circles. But, this was a conflict of interest which was very bad for business. I was going to have to talk to Chantelle about that. She was the one who'd referred her to begin with. I didn't have time to unravel a Jerry Springer plot. All I wanted was make my money and run my business smoothly.

I was so deep in thought I hadn't noticed Amanda had wandered off. I looked to my left and then my right, she was nowhere to be found. She was too drunk not to be in my eyesight, so I left the dart table looking for her. I found her damn near glued to a gentleman at the bar.

I walked up slowly ready to pull her away when I got a glimpse of his face. He was the mystery man that showed up on my date with the German. My heart skipped a beat and suddenly I felt as if I couldn't swallow. I wanted to say something, but was at a loss for words. He smiled at me lifting up his glass as if to say cheers. I didn't make any moves I only watched.

"So," he started. "Is this your friend you were telling me about?" he asked, looking at me with those beady little eyes.

Amanda was right. She wasn't cut out for this line of work. She totally missed the energy that was emanating between me and her newfound friend. She went to introduce us and to his surprise, I held out my hand, smiling giving him a firm handshake.

This time he had a chance to be caught off guard. The initial shock had worn off and the buzz from the vodka I'd been slamming took over.

"Nice to meet you..." I said, leaving things open for him to introduce himself.

"His name is Oleg," Amanda chimed in smiling.

"Well Oleg," I said, returning his sneaky glare with one of my own. "I'm sure spending some time with my friend here would prove to be worth your while. Give us a call sometime and we can make those arrangements for you." I grinned, handing him one of my GFE Inc. cards.

He took the card smiling as he rolled the square piece of paper between his fingers. "That sounds like a plan Ms...."

"Claudia," I responded dryly.

"Yes," he said, looking down at the card as if he were reading it. "That's right, Claudia."

I grabbed hold of Amanda's arm, pulling her out the door. She was as drunk as a skunk whining halfway home until I told her to shut the hell up. I needed to think. So he wanted Amanda? I wasn't sure how she'd feel about going on another date but I'd definitely make it worth her while.

"Amanda," I started before looking over noticing that she was fast asleep. It was better that I spoke to her about Oleg when she was sober anyway. Despite the bullshit, I had a pretty lucky night. All kinds of valuable information had presented itself to me. I needed to get in touch with Chantelle and Lacey to get them up to speed on what was going on.

After I made sure Amanda was safe and secure in her apartment, I headed out calling motor mouth first.

"Lacey, I need you and Chantelle either at the office or at my apartment ASAP," I said.

"Well that's going to be a problem," Lacey responded. I asked her why. "Because, Chantelle is with a client." She responded as if I should've known.

"No, I looked at the schedule earlier today and she only had three dates today and they were in the daytime." I said confused. We worked as a team. Each of us did our part to ensure every girls safety and security. We also had to keep each other abreast of our comings and goings. There were plenty crazies looking to do bad things to girls like us. We had to stay safe.

"She had a late request. I've been calling and texting you all day." She added.

I looked down at my phone and she had. I'd forgotten to turn the volume back on after leaving the courthouse. I was so wrapped up with Amanda, Victor, and Loretta's shit I had neglected to stay on top of my business. I cursed myself before asking Lacey to meet up with me.

"I can't tonight," she responded.

"Why?" I shot. "What do you have to do?" I questioned.

"Contrary to what you guys believe Tawny, I do have a life you know," she shot back. I was being very inconsiderate. Sometimes I could be damn selfish, but the truth was I tried to keep someone around at all times. I just didn't want to be alone.

I walked into GFE, Inc.'s small office to find Miranda sitting at her desk watching Netflix on her laptop. She was our overnight client service agent.

"Hey," she said, closing her laptop shut. I waved my hand, telling her that it was ok how else was she going to work third shift in the office by herself. She smiled, letting out a sigh of relief.

"Are you okay?" she asked inquisitively. I opted not to answer her as I retrieved two glasses and a bottle of vodka from my office. I came out sitting the items on her desk as I pulled up a chair.

"So how's it been going?" I asked. This was the first time I'd ever really spoken to her. Not because I was a bitch of an employer, but because I'd just been so busy. She was hired after it was determined that we couldn't do everything on our own. I'd honestly been meaning to sit down with her for a long time.

"It's going great," she answered sincerely. "I really appreciate you giving me this opportunity."

I nodded my head and smiled, pouring a small shot of vodka and pushing it towards her.

"I'm sorry," she responded. "I don't drink." She added pointing to the sobriety pen she was wearing on her shirt. I felt like an asshole. I apologized, but she was ok with it. For the next two or three hours I put a pretty large dent in the bottle I'd taken out of my office. Miranda and I talked about her kids and being a single mom etc.

If I hadn't known any better I would've thought she was around our age. She was a seasoned woman and had been through a lot. The stories she told she'd called her "testimony". I wasn't sure what that meant, but I listened anyway. Despite her over religiousness, she was a pretty cool woman.

"This could be out of line and you can tell me it's none of my business if you choose," she said. "But, if you ever find yourself needing someone to talk to without any judgment, and that can keep a secret, you know where I'm at." She smiled. I appreciated that coming from her.

CHAPTER EIGHT

Daddy had called and told me he needed to see me right away. When I pulled up to the house I saw all my siblings' cars sitting out front. Even my mother's car was in the driveway. I couldn't imagine why everyone was over there. Or even why daddy felt like I needed to be around them.

My mother and I never got along. She was an evil manipulative bitch. She never actually hit on me, but she'd do little things to let me know that she didn't like me much. I always thought it was because she was jealous of the relationship my dad and I had. Imagine that, your own mother being jealous of you.

After I became a teen I really stopped trying to please her. The relationship she'd had with my father was going downhill anyway. He'd had children by other women and she wasn't doing much better. She was cheating also. They were together out of habit.

I hated seeing my dad unhappy with her so when they split it didn't bother me. There wasn't a battle over custody because she didn't want me. I didn't want her either. To be honest, she didn't do anything. None of the women daddy chose to be with did. They were all bums dependent on him for everything. Their children were the same way.

They always had their hand out like he was their own personal ATM machine. I didn't even ask for that much and I was his favorite. When my sister Augustine came to live with us after her mother died she was the worst. She would play on daddy's intelligence so she could have whatever she wanted.

He'd tell me that she was just "going through something" because her mom had died. Her mother wasn't coming back so *why was she so upset anyway? Her crying and daddy trying to appease her was bullshit. She just needed to get over it. He told me I needed to have more compassion. We'd gotten into this huge argument because I refused. That was the first time my dad had ever called me selfish. I never stopped loving and adoring him, but his words changed the entire dynamic of our relationship.*

I allowed him to cater to Augustine in her time of need without any interference. When he attempted to include me in things they had going on I'd decline. I continued to do everything that I normally did, except I made it a point to do it extremely well. When I had a problem I figured them out on my own.

For my sweet 16 I didn't ask daddy for anything. I busted my ass babysitting, mowing lawns, designing and sewing custom made prom dresses for my peers, and I'd even sold marijuana every now and then. I did all that so he'd never have to worry about doing anything for me. Maybe I was being selfish and immature, but who cared.

My daddy didn't become a millionaire sitting on his ass. I wasn't going to become one by asking him for handouts. I damn sure wasn't going to become dependent on him for my very existence. I was a lot like him with the exception of being weak. I didn't have ties with people that would cost me my happiness. He spent all that time trying to make Augustine happy and what did she go and do? She hung herself. Yep, she'd killed herself in the basement.

He was devastated by that. For some reason he blamed himself thinking he could've done anything for her. Instead of consoling him I allowed him to be. I stayed out of his way to let him sort through whatever feelings he needed to sort through. That was when Victor started showing me extra attention.

Before long the affection I got from daddy, I was able to get him. Only this relationship was better. Victor not only made me smile, he made my entire body feel good. I started spending less and less time with daddy. He really needed that space. He never tried to tell me otherwise. So I did whatever I wanted.

Later he confessed that maybe he'd gone about helping Augustine in the wrong way. I wanted to tell him that both she and her mother were destined for death. They were just dreary people. They were sad for no reason at all. Some people you just can't help. No matter how much you'd want to make them happy if they don't want happiness they're not going to get it. Instead, I listened as he vocalized his "failure" to protect his "baby". Then I left.

When I walked into the house it looked as if everyone had been crying. My heart started to pound rapidly as I scanned the room for my dad. I didn't see his face. I could feel little beads of sweat forming on my forehead. I closed my eyes, inhaling deeply before opening them again to see my father walking towards me.

I was still nervous as hell but relieved to see him. I looked at him asking what was going. He ushered me to sit down telling me he had to talk to me. Everyone was staring. I didn't know what was going on but I was sure I was going to find out soon. My mother walked over to me placing her arm around my shoulder. Since when did she ever want to comfort me? I hadn't seen nor spoken with her in 7 months.

I moved her hand from my back looking at my dad for answers. He took a deep breath before allowing the words to roll off of his tongue. I was taken aback for a moment. I shook my head from side to side, closing my eyes. Daddy was still talking, but everything sounded slow. I took my hands rubbing them over my face, then through my hair.

I placed my hands in my lap noticing there were traces of eyeliner and eye shadow on the palm of my hand. I didn't care. I sat there silent, calm, and stoic. It was as if everyone in the house attempted to talk to me at once.

Their voices seemed to get louder and louder until I yelled for them all to shut up. I refused to discuss anything in front of them. I didn't consider them my family. Why had they even called me over there for that? They all were very aware that I wanted nothing to do with them.

"Daddy, I'm going to come back later so we can talk in private," I said, not acknowledging anyone else in the room.

Of course, my brother Josh had to say something. He always had something to say. The old 30 year old professional student aka bum always had the answers.

"Tawny, we need to deal with this as a family." He said.

"And tell me again why you think you need to advise me on anything Josh," I responded sarcastically. That was all I needed to say before everyone in the room started going back and forth. Even my mother had joined in. I looked over at my dad who was rubbing the bridge of his nose. His head was tilted downwards as he tried to tune out everything that was going on.

I almost felt sorry for him, but then I thought why? He was the one who chose to have all these kids by random women. The more I looked at the circus act of a family I had the more pissed off I became. I tried to head towards the door, leaving them all to sort through their thoughts and feelings together, but my mother grabbed hold of my arm.

"Sweetheart we're all here for you," she assured me through pleading eyes. I almost believed her until I remembered that she'd never really been a significant part of my life. I snatched my arm away telling her to go to hell.

Why did I say that? Everyone in the room was now yelling at me. They told me how spoiled and selfish I was. My sister even had the nerve to say that I was childish. That was a joke considering the fact that she'd had two children by her loser boyfriend who left her and daddy was footing all of her bills. I let her know just that.

That really got them going. Everyone was yelling out something. All while my dad just sat there quietly with my mother rubbing his back gently. I didn't like the look of that. What in the hell did they have going on? I rolled my eyes turning my back on everyone. I would discuss this with my dad on my time not theirs. I hopped in my car speeding off and down the street.

My siblings started to call my phone back to back. I ignored several of their calls before turning it completely off. I sighed, getting lost in my thoughts.

HONK! HONK! HONK! I was snapped out of my daze by the blaring horn of a truck that just missed hitting me. I was so wrapped up in my own head that I'd run the red light. I pulled over to the side of the road slapping my steering wheel. One hit led to another before I was consistently pounding into it. When I couldn't hit it any longer I sat there chest rising as I heaved in anger.

I hated not being in control. I hated feeling like I didn't have options. I was helpless in this situation. I needed some serious retail therapy. I merged back onto the road headed towards the mall.

It was a Saturday, so the mall was packed as usual. I was relieved that I'd put on my sneakers and workout gear earlier with the anticipation of heading to the gym. That's where I should've gone, so I could hit that bag a few times to let off some steam.

I walked through the crowd heading towards my favorite department store.

"Tawny!" I could hear someone yelling my name. I looked around, but didn't see anyone so I kept on going. I really didn't feel like being bothered anyway. I increased my speed ducking off into a small boutique to get out of sight. I was sorting through a rack of pants when Miranda came walking up behind me out of breath.

"I knew that was you," she said, smiling showing a set of perfectly straight teeth. I looked at her and smiled. I couldn't help it her attitude was kind of contagious.

"Well who is this?" I asked, touching the hand of the small little girl she was holding in her arms.

"This is my granddaughter Olivia," she smiled before looking around and adding, "My daughters are around here somewhere."

I smiled not knowing what to say. She had failed to mention that one of her teenaged daughters had a child. But, I guess it shouldn't have been that big of a surprise. Kids were having kids often these days.

"Well she's very gorgeous," I managed to smile before continuing on with small talk. Before long Miranda, Olivia, and I was strolling through the mall from store to store having a great time. She wasn't someone I'd have chosen to hang around on my own, but I was actually having a lot of fun.

We somehow found ourselves in a children's store and before I knew it Olivia and three bags of clothes were in my hands. Miranda had insisted on me not purchasing anything for her grand baby, but I couldn't help it. She was too cute. Her innocence took me to a place I hadn't been in a long time.

As we rode the escalator downstairs we were greeted by her daughters. They were two beautiful young ladies. Despite the youngest of the two having had a child she was extremely respectful and intelligent. She didn't fit the description of how I thought a teenaged mother would be. Then again, that would make me a bigot to believe her to be any way at all without getting to know her. I secretly scolded myself for even thinking such thoughts.

My smiles quickly turned into a frown when I found myself face to face with Ryan. I'd managed not to run into him for months and now here we were face to face in the middle of the mall.

"Hey," he smiled with his hands in his pocket looking uncomfortable. Miranda could obviously feel the tension between the two because she told me she and the girls were going to go get something to eat. She grabbed Olivia and they disappeared into the crowd. Ryan and I stood there looking at one another without saying a word.

"Listen," he started before I cut him off by telling him that he owed me no explanation. "But, I do owe you an apology."

I looked at him like he was crazy. "No you don't owe me a thing." I assured him. I wasn't sure what his problem was but there was nothing we needed to talk about ever.

"Ok," he said searching for something else to say. I decided to take that opportunity to keep moving. He was causing me to feel closed in. Ryan and I had enough ups and downs I wanted to leave my past just where it was in the past.

"Wait," he said running behind me grabbing my arm. When I turned around to curse him out he leaned forward kissing me long and hard. We stood there for what seemed like an eternity locked at the lips.

Next thing I knew we had snuck into the restroom of a very upscale department store. I pressed him against the wall tugging at his jeans. I finally got them unbuttoned sliding onto my knees. I pulled out his thick muscle and begin to softly suck on the head. He let out a slight moan resting his hand on top of my head.

Inch by inch I took him into my mouth until I began to gag. I swallowed him until my eyes watered. That turned me on even more. His moans became louder when I started to juggle his balls in the palm of my hand. My tongue twisted and turned as I pushed forward devouring him like my life depended on it.

He gripped the sides of the stall as if he was going to cum. He wasn't getting off that easy. There would be no coming. At least not at that time. I slowly stood stroking his dick as I stared him in his eyes.

"Fuck me," I said between gritted teeth. I slid out of my shoes and pants quickly ready to feel him deep inside me. He lifted me up in the air, allowing me to wrap my legs around him. My pussy swallowed him as he slid himself inside of me standing there for a moment basking in a glory only he knew.

I tightened my walls around him and begin to move on my own. I needed to be fucked. He started to meet me with hard thrusts sending shards of pain and pleasure throughout my entire body. I clawed at his back as my body started to stiffen. I was going to cum.

His thrusts were becoming shorter and faster. I moaned loudly. I was going to cum. Like old times we both let go together. He stood there for a moment holding me his head buried between my breasts. I didn't know how to feel I was kind of numb.

"My dad has cancer," I said. I wasn't sure why, maybe because he was familiar and I still trusted him, but I just blurted it out. His head popped up as he stared at me. Only thing is I wasn't sure why he was staring. Was it for compassion or because he could see I didn't feel anything.

CHAPTER NINE

"No I'm not going on the call!" Chantelle said clearly irritated that I'd even suggested she come.

"And why is that?" I asked with my arms folded. She was starting to become a serious pain in my ass. I didn't know what was going on with her, but she'd become a lot more bitchy than usual.

"What because I'm black you think I want to go on dates with thugs?" she asked sarcastically.

"Are you serious?" She was unbelievable. What did black have to do with entertaining one of the hottest rappers in the world? Money was money it didn't matter where it was coming from. What in the hell did she think he was going to make her do?

"Yes, I'm very serious," Chantelle replied, causing me to shake my head. I turned to walk away, but she grabbed my arm. I was really getting tired of people grabbing my arm lately. I pulled loose from her grip.

We both stood there glaring at each other until Lacey came between us. She started to remind us that we'd been best friends for far too long to have any type of falling out.

"Well you tell this bitch that." Chantelle responded. I wanted to slap her, but I refused to stoop to her level. She'd been acting very funny lately and I had so many other things on my mind than to be worried about her little attitude. I had yet to tell the two girls I considered to be sisters about my dad because I'd never found the time.

Hell I'd been taking him to his treatments for the past several weeks praying for a miracle. I sighed, hating that

Chantelle and I had just gotten into such a heated argument. I went to apologize, but she cut me off telling me I'd always thought I was better than them. I asked her who them was. She said she and Lacey.

I looked at her and then at Lacey, who shrugged her shoulders. Oh so did she feel that way too? Chantelle had a wild look in her eyes and I knew something was up. I wanted to slap myself for not noticing before.

"Are you fucking high?" I asked walking up to her and looking at her face. Her pupils were dilated, her mouth twitched, I knew she was tweaking. She didn't answer as Lacey and I stared at one another.

"No, no, no, no," Lacey said starting to panic. "We've got to get you some help." She said as tears started rolling down her face. I should've taken Chantelle to the side because Lacey couldn't handle "issues". She wasn't built for adversity and we'd always kept her protected as if she was our little sister.

"Calm down," I said softly, trying to maintain my cool. I didn't know what she'd been taking lately or why, but it was affecting her character big time.

Chantelle refused to talk to me or Lacey for that matter. The more I tried to talk to her, the more agitated she became so I decided to just leave her alone. When she was sober, we could talk. Trying to do so right now would just cause drama. I'd had enough of that going on in my life.

"I'm out of here," Chantelle said snatching up her bag heading towards the door. Lacey and I looked on in silence.

"Is she going to be ok?" Lacey asked looking worried to death. I didn't bother to answer that question either. Situations like that were sticky. It all really depended on the person and what fate had in store for them. This time Lacey wasn't taking my silence as an opportunity to just leave it alone.

"I'm calling Mr. Jackson," she said, pulling out her cell phone which I snatched from her.

"You're calling Mr. Jackson to tell him what, Lacey?" I asked. Before she called Mr. Jackson about Chantelle's drug problem we needed to evaluate the entire situation.

"That she needs help Tawny," Lacey responded, as if I should've been well aware of what she meant. I was aware. Now just wasn't the time to narc on our friend.

"Not now," I responded calmly.

"I'm sorry Tawny but I refuse to let her slip through the cracks and become a drug addict because you think now isn't the time!" Lacey shot back catching me off guard. She never went against the grain. Lacey always chose my side, but this time she was choosing her own. I took a deep breath before asking her nicely to just wait until we had a chance to talk to her. For all we knew that was Chantelle's first dance with the "devil".

It took a few more minutes of convincing but I got Lacey to agree we should talk to our friend first. Plus it had been months since the two had even spoken to one another. Chantelle still hadn't told us why Mr. Jackson had cut her off to begin with. Hell, her drug problem could've very well been the reason. Just because we'd just found out about it didn't mean that it hadn't been going on for quite some time.

I hated that we'd started keeping secrets from one another. Keeping secrets were proving to be just as bad as telling lies. I felt like now was a good time to tell Lacey about my dad, when two of the most beautiful women I'd ever seen in my life walked through GFE Inc.'s doors.

"Excuse me can I help you?" I asked not knowing who they were, why they were in our office, or how they even knew this was an office.

"We're here for the audition," the Hispanic one said smiling. I had completely forgotten that I had two ladies coming in that day. Judging by the looks of the two we were going to be making a whole lot of money with those two. Lacey forced a smile on her face asking them what they called themselves.

"I'm Cynful and this is Pepper," the Hispanic said. Pepper wasted no time turning on their music, they meant business. They were trained to go, I liked them already.

Their hips began to move ticking from one side to the next along with the beat. And then their backsides bounced ridiculously fast unlike anything I'd ever seen before. They moved their bodies in ways I would never even attempt to do. Not because I didn't have rhythm, but because twerking was not my specialty. What they were doing was nothing short of amazing. I was sold!

They'd come right on time because I needed someone to come to the 11 o'clock I had that night. I knew those guys were used to ladies who could shake their ass like that so it was on. I offered them a contract. They happily accepted. Lacey quickly began preparing their paperwork.

"So would you ladies be interested in joining me tonight?" I asked, sure they wouldn't turn down the offer. "I've got a very high profile client who is looking to have some fun." I smiled.

The ladies looked at each other then asked me who my client was. I told them the name Pepper nearly fell out of her chair.

"You've got to be kidding me," Pepper said, speaking for the first time. I assured her I was not and that we'd need to start getting ready very soon. They were amped and ready to sign on the dotted line. That was fine since I was all about making money. Eagerness in this business could take them a long way.

Lacey collected their ID's while I gave them a tour of the office. When I took them to the "Glam" room their mouths opened in awe. I smiled knowing that we'd done a good job. The room was decorated solely in gold. It wasn't gaudy, just elegant. We had a section set up for makeup and hair, costumes, floor to ceiling mirrors had been installed, as well as a place to shower just for times like these.

Pepper was drawn to a turquoise gypsy costume. I smiled as she ran her hand over the fabric allowing her fingers to slide through the fringes.

"Do you like that?" I asked.

"Oh yeah," Pepper responded not even bothering to look my way. "This is hot."

"Go ahead. It's yours then."

She looked at me like I couldn't have been serious, but I was as serious as a heart attack. Pepper took a glance at Cyn who had a frown plastered across her face.

"No, I can't take this." She responded, removing her hands from the material.

"And why is that?" I inquired not sure what was really going on.

"Because, we don't take handouts, we came here to work," Cyn responded for her. Cynful was going to be a tough cookie to crack. She had trust issues, but truth was I could be trusted. I didn't want anything but the best for my girls. As long as they were happy so was I.

"Well," Lacey jumped in as she came through the door handing each our newest

"Girlfriends" back their identification cards. "The thing is this is not a handout."

"Then what do you like to call it?" Cyn asked defiantly.

"First and foremost were you ladies expecting to go meet with one of the world's biggest entertainers dressed like that?" she asked, motioning towards the outfits they'd come to audition in. They looked ok and they could most definitely dance, but they looked cheap. The girls looked at one another and then looked over themselves.

"Although we work for you," Lacey continued. "You represent the GFE Incorporated brand. Our brand consists of only the most talented, beautiful, and classy women in this portion of the US. We have ladies in 7 different states. This organization is our livelihood and now yours. So consider these as gifts of appreciation and our being grateful to have invested in you. We have faith in your cause because you have faith in ours." I smiled watching Lacey work her magic.

If anyone ever had reservations it was always Lacey that eased their minds. She was someone they could go to. Soft spoken and even motherly in a sense, but she knew how to get things to go the way she needed them to.

Cyn's shoulders dropped a bit as she made her way over to the wardrobe section. She was drawn to an Aztec Warrior outfit. She held the one piece up to her tanned skin, closing her eyes as she inhaled deeply. She opened her eyes staring at herself in the mirror. They sparkled underneath the light. She had the hustlers' spirit.

"What kind of fabric is this?" she asked.

"Silk," I responded.

"Where did you find this?" she asked. "I've never seen anything like it."

I smiled telling her that our partner Chantelle was our seamstress. She stayed up many of nights when she wasn't working designing new costumes for the business. I assured them they would meet her soon omitting the drama that had erupted earlier. They were in utter amazement. I'd known Chantelle, my entire life and she'd always had an eye for fashion.

We called in hair and makeup, got dressed and were on our way to the hotel to meet up with Magik in no time. The limo ride was deafeningly quiet. I could tell they were nervous. That was how it was for most people their first time. Once things got started all of the tension would cease and it would become second nature to them. Nurturing was something that came naturally to most women. That was exactly what our clients needed to feel like they were the only thing that mattered.

"You ladies ok over there?" I asked breaking the silence. They both looked at me before Cyn responded that she was fine. Pepper looked less sure of herself. Leaning forward I placed my hand on her leg assuring her that it would be ok. For a moment she reminded me of a lost little girl. My heart actually started to go out to her. I had to catch myself from being too mushy. I knew what came with this lifestyle but the fact remained we still had to live. I brushed that instinct off and began my pep talk.

I told them about my first time and all the success stories of their colleagues. Money was the motive and after explaining to them how much could be made, it seemed as if they were amped again. When the car stopped we had to have our game faces on.

"Remember," I encouraged. "If you don't believe in what you're here for they won't either," I reminded them before stating to keep their chins up, and shoulders back. They nodded in agreement. Despite my brief reservations as soon as we exited the vehicle Pepper and Cyn were ready to play the game.

We strutted through the hotel lobby like we owned the place. Men and women gawked as we pretended not to notice making our way through to the elevators. I hit the 30th floor. The ride was silent, all of us in our own thoughts as we ascended to the top. That was how I wanted to think of it. If this went right GFE Incorporated would be on an entirely different level than any other service in the state.

When the elevator doors opened a cloud of smoke crept towards us like fog. The entire floor was filled with people laughing, talking, and fucking. Yes fucking in the hallway. If those ho's weren't so raunchy they could've been a part of GFE and made some cash off their trade. But, I couldn't see myself working with any female who didn't know how to present herself in environments such as this.

The groupies who had camped out in the hotel waiting for Magik's tour bus to arrive were giving us dirty looks. I could tell that my new little ladies weren't feeling too comfortable.

"I'm 'bout to slap one of these bitches," I heard Pepper say to Cyn. I slowed my stride so Pepper could catch up.

"No you're not," I smiled. "Bask in all your glory. We are the paid entertainment and they are the cheap thrill, big difference." I stated never taking my eyes off of our surroundings. I was searching for the Magik man himself and it wasn't too long before I found him.

CHAPTER TEN

When Magik's eyes met mine there were no words spoken just pleasant smiles. Had he not been a client, I could've made him mine. I'd never dated a black man before, but this guy looked good. He had milk chocolate skin, the perfect smile, his features were very exotic. Although he was young as hell his entire persona was just what I probably needed in my life. However, with the drama that was going with Victor and Ryan I didn't need to add any extra baggage to that claim.

"And you must be Claudia," he said, taking my hand and twirling me around in a complete circle.

"That would be me," I responded appreciating the attention I was receiving from my newfound "money machine." "And these," I added gesturing towards Cyn and Pepper. "These two lovely ladies are my friends Cynful and Pepper." I added. As if on cue, they did a little prance before bringing their hands to their hips and smiling. After our introductions and small talk we made our way into the restroom to get preparing for the night.

"Oh my God!" Pepper said giving Cyn a high five. "I can't believe that we in here 'bout to kick it wit' Magik!"

"Yeah, I know!" Cyn responded in her thick accent smiling genuinely for the first time.

I laughed at their greenness. They ranted and raved about how nervous they were putting him a pedestal. Which, I could understand. He was a sexy man who had a whole lot of money, but he wasn't anymore extraordinary than them.

"I'm glad you two are here," I began. For some reason this time I had their full attention. "I want you ladies to remember never to see yourself as ordinary. Not with your clients or anyone else." I told them.

They seemed to be shocked at what I had just said. Pepper began to sound off Magik's credentials like he was the Messiah or something. While the things he'd managed to accomplish were impressive, he was human.

"What is that supposed to mean?" Cyn asked.

"It means that your being here is extraordinary. The process of conception that created you was extraordinary. The air that fills your lungs and keeps you alive is extraordinary. When your mother gave birth to you it was extraordinary. Every trial, tribulation, milestone, and plateau you reach is extraordinary." I had their attention and I could see that they were getting my point. "So don't get star struck show him that you are the real prize. Let him know why he has to pay the big bucks to be in your presence. Make sure your ego is bigger than his while making him feel like he is on top." I added looking at my face in the mirror.

The girls nodded as they slid into their outfits. We all looked in the mirror. We looked pretty damn good. We were ready to go. We opened the door and there sat Magik along with six other fellows.

"Here we go," Cyn mumbled under her breath before doing something I never thought I'd see her do. She walked over to each man running her fingers across their faces. She made her way to the front of the room surrounded by men on all sides and began to move her body in a circle. Her ass bounced up and down displaying only the bottom of her cheeks. She was dancing to her own music.

The men seemed to be enticed. She had their full attention. I noticed Pepper and Magik exchanging looks and smiles. They were natural charmers, mesmerizing even. One of the guys turned on the music drowning out all of the commotion that was taking place outside.

Pepper slowly made her way to Cyn's side bending down on her knees rubbing her hands all over the Hispanic beauty. I saw one of the guys adjusting his dick in his pants. I chuckled on the inside.

They were fully clothed, but the sensuality of the acts they were committing to one another was enough to turn anyone on. I stood there rocking from side to side enjoying the show myself.

Cyn turned to me motioning me with her finger to come closer. For the first time since I met them, I allowed them to take the lead. They danced around me like I was a supreme goddess allowing their hands to roam all over my body. I was Aphrodite for the night and they were worshipping me.

Cyn stood behind me lifting my shirt over my head as Pepper pulled my skirt down exposing my pretty pink pussy. The room was quiet but loud. The weed smoke continued to swarm through the air, giving us a sexy high. When they were done teasing me by going just far enough to entice our audience the dynamic changed and Pepper were our focus of attention.

Her dark skin and tight body were what women could only dream of having. She bit down on her lip while I rubbed her nipples making them erect. Cyn was palming her ass, smacking, then kissing it as she moaned. I was starting to think these girls had done this before. Magik and I exchanged glances as he mouthed thank you.

Pepper was fully nude with Cyn dominating her. I allowed them to have their moment pleasing each other until they both came simultaneously. The men in the room were the complete opposite of what I would've imagined them being. Maybe they were used to this type of thing, but they waited their turn.

We made sure that the wait wasn't in vain. Pepper wasted no time making her way to Magik, who'd been eyeballing her all night. He was intoxicated by her beauty. They disappeared into a door on the side of the room. I knew she was getting her money's worth and her rocks off.

Cyn and I played our position. There were dicks pulled out everywhere. We went down the line licking, sucking, jacking every last one of them. When it was time to fuck that was exactly what we did. We could've made a porno out of that scene. *Your Girlfriend Loves Being*

Gangbanged. It was a great experience to say the least.

Cyn and Pepper were grinning from ear to ear as we reloaded the limo. I could tell they felt accomplished. I'd have felt accomplished too we'd all made a nice piece of change for three hours of work.

"I can't believe this shit!" Pepper yelled as we were driving off from the hotel. "That was the easiest money I've ever made in my life!" she boasted.

"Yeah," Cyn agreed. "It was cool. I really can't complain." She added not seeming too fazed by the amount of money she'd just made. None the less she agreed to have had a good time. It actually seemed like that was all she was looking for, was a good time. I was glad that the experience hadn't scared them away. Although all of their dates were different they were definitely going to leave with a pocketbook full of cash.

My cell phone started ringing drawing my attention away from the pair.

"Hey Lacey, what's up?" I sang into the receiver. It was pretty late, so I knew it had to be about business.

"Wait hold on," I responded putting my hand over the receiver asking Pepper and Cyn to lower their voices and turn down the music. "She did what?!" I screamed into the receiver.

This had to be a dream. Chantelle would never make such a stupid and irrational decision. Then again, she was high when she'd left us and was clearly capable of doing and saying anything. Cyn and Pepper looked at me with inquiring eyes. I told Lacey I'd call her back. I told the ladies I had a family matter to tend to and had the driver drop them off to their car at the office.

As soon as the limo took off I called Lacey back. "Where are you guys?" I asked feeling emotional. She told me to meet them at her condo.

Lacey had always been the most dramatic of the trio so when she said things were bad I took that with a grain of salt. Walking into Lacey's home and seeing

142

my best friend made me almost drop to my knees. My usual tough exterior slowly deteriorated as I looked at her body. Her face was swollen almost beyond recognition. I wondered if it would ever look the same.

The cuts, bruises, and burn marks seemed to cover every inch of her body. Her long thick and kinky hair was matted to the left side with blood. I couldn't tell if there was blood coming from her ears or somewhere else.

"She won't let me call the police," Lacey said softly with tears flowing freely from her eyes.

"Well she doesn't have a damn choice." I responded taking out my phone and dialing 9-1-. Chantelle jumped up from her position on the couch knocking my phone and me to the ground.

"You're not calling anybody," she responded breathing heavily. I looked at her like she was insane. In that moment I believe she had to have been. Clearly she wasn't thinking straight. I didn't dare challenge her at that moment. She needed me to be her friend. I needed to go about the situation in an entirely different fashion.

"Then what do you want us to do Chantelle?" I asked her through pleading eyes. "Who in the hell did this to you?" I demanded, feeling grieved and angered. She looked away as if she was embarrassed to say. I wouldn't call the police but I was going to find out who'd beaten her like that.

"I don't know," she responded avoiding eye contact. I wasn't taking that, however. She knew damn well who'd done that to her. I knew when she was lying.

"Dammit Chantelle!" I yelled, causing both her and Lacey to jump. "Tell me what happened?"

I'd never yelled at either one of my friends but enough was enough. I was dealing with too much at the moment. They both sat there in silence, neither one of them choosing to look at me. I tried to play tough but on the inside I was afraid. Maybe we weren't doing the right thing with GFE Inc. Maybe all of this was because we were absolutely doing the wrong thing.

I took a deep breath to calm myself down. I told Chantelle I was going to ask her one more time and I needed her to tell me the truth.

"I've been going on my own dates," she said through deep heartfelt sobs. Lacey looked at me as I shook my head in disappointment. However, I wasn't disappointed enough to even be worried about business at that time. I just needed to know what our next move should've been.

"The other night, Miranda was running late and I was in the office." She started. As her story came together so did the pieces to this puzzle. I started to think about the experience that got my friends involved in this industry in the first place.

"They were really nice guys. Said they were in town on business from Germany. The first date went great. I don't know what happened this time." She started to sob uncontrollably. "I lost control of the situation. I'm Lady Heroin!" she screamed out.

My blood began to boil as I envisioned Lutz and Oleg torturing my friend in the same way they'd tortured me. I had to remain calm and level headed. Things never worked out when you acted on impulse, especially dealing with men who had a little bit of power. We were the daughters of men with that same type of power. We saw firsthand what money could buy you.

"You don't want to call the police right?" I asked calmly. Chantelle nodded her head. "What about your dad?" I asked seriously.

Both Chantelle and Lacey's eyes grew as big as saucers at the mention of Mr. Jackson.

"No, I don't want him to know anything!" Chantelle insisted. I wasn't sure how true it had been, but her father was a known gangster in our area. The rumor was, he a big time kingpin who laundered money through multiple businesses in five different states.

Just then my phone rang, it was Cyn. I started not to answer it, but it could've been important. Walking out of the room and into the bathroom, I hit talk.

"You left pretty quickly is everything alright with you?" I didn't know rather to say everything was fine or break down crying. "Are you there?" she asked, breaking my train of thought. I was never at a loss for words, but right then I had nothing to say. I mumbled things were fine and I'd call her back shortly. She told me if I needed anything that she was just a phone call away.

It was something about the way she'd said those words that prompted me to ask her to meet me at the diner down the street. She didn't hesitate. She could be there in fifteen minutes. Lacey had given Chantelle some pain pills before I'd gotten there and she was now falling asleep. I whispered that I'd be returning shortly and not to let Chantelle leave. Lacey assured me that she wasn't going anywhere.

She'd quickly dozed off and was snoring lightly in spite of the amount of pain she had to have been feeling.

"Where are you going?" Lacey whispered, walking me to the door. I told her I had to handle some business. She looked at me funny. "GFE business?" she asked looking worried.

"No." I responded simply.

"I'm starting to rethink this whole GFE thing," she blurted out shaken by the entire ordeal.

"Just calm down," I said softly. "I'm going to handle it." I responded.

"Handle it?" Lacey laughed. "This is what you promised from the beginning Tawny! That everyone would be safe and this was a good thing for all of us! But it's not. Do you see our friend in there?" I knew that she was scared and upset so I just allowed her to have that moment to vent. In the right time I would explain to her what all comes with this business. She would understand that these things happened and were a casualty of war.

She'd have a choice either to be in or out. Either way I'd still love her and support her decision.

"I'll see you in a few," I responded, before walking out the door. I started my car sitting there for a moment caught up in my thoughts. So much had been going wrong in such little time I was becoming overwhelmed. Everything hitting me at once from my dad, to Chantelle, Victor, the Germans, Ryan, my head was spinning. My life no longer felt like my own. I sighed, glancing in my rearview. *That white car had been tailing me for the past three blocks.*

CHAPTER ELEVEN

I sat there in front of the two Hispanic men wringing my hands one over the other. I didn't know why I was so intimidated, but I was. The nervousness was there. Cyn had assured me that her uncles were very good people. Upon meeting them, I smiled nervously. I'd never been in contact with men of their stature. From what I'd heard on the news and in movies I wasn't so sure I'd made the right decision to even become involved.

She promised me not to say anything about her working for GFE. I wasn't sure what that was all about, but then again I got it. No one wanted to be labeled a whore, especially by their uncles.

I kept my word and pretended to be a good friend of hers.

Jesus and Luis were men of very few words, but the things that came out of their mouths spoke volumes. Even my normal charm was overlooked, according to their demeanor. I had no choice than to respect who they were. The night I met Cyn at the diner against my better judgment, I let it all out. In doing that I felt as if I'd made a friend. Maybe she had too.

"My niece tells me that you have a foreign problem of some sort?" Luis inquired, as he leaned in towards me. I wanted to say no I don't and just leave, but I couldn't move. My mouth wouldn't open, my head wouldn't nod, it was as if I was stuck in time.

Jesus looked at his brother, then at Cyn. Luis held his hand up nodding his head as if he understood what was going on.

"You think maybe you and I should speak in private?" he asked, looking directly into my blue eyes. I nodded my head yes, even though I didn't think that was going to make too much of a difference. For some reason I was still afraid. Not that they'd done anything to make me feel such a way. It was their presence alone that let me know who they were and what they were about.

I closed my eyes speaking to myself through thoughts. I needed to calm myself down. I didn't want to make this man angry or worse uncomfortable with my uncomfortableness. I waited for the duo to leave before I opened my mouth to speak.

"Thank you so much for meeting with me," I started. My voice was a bit rocky, but I continued on. "I spoke with Cyn and she thinks, very highly of you and thought that you could help me solve a little problem I'm having." I continued nervously. As I spoke Luis stared at me intensely holding onto every word that came from my mouth.

When I finally took the chance to look him in his eyes however they weren't as hard as I expected to be. They slightly put me at ease. When I was done explaining the line of business I was in and what had happened to myself and Chantelle I was able to exhale.

We sat there in silence for a moment before Luis asked how I thought he could help me. Hell I didn't know maybe kill the bastards. I didn't dare let that slip out of my mouth. I sat there considering his question.

"I want you to think long and hard, Tawny Sinclair," he stated catching me off guard. I didn't know how in the hell he knew my last name. That alone sent the chills up my spine. I felt like he was warning me that the next words that came out of my mouth had better been right. I sat there for what seemed like an eternity until my mind connected with my brain.

"All I need is back up just in case anything goes wrong." I responded more boldly than I was feeling. Luis smiled nodding his head. "I only need muscle." I continued lying, but anticipating on doing whatever it took to make my words the truth.

Luis laughed, causing my own lips to spread. I was blushing. He assured me

153

that any friend of Cyn's was a friend of his and if that was all I needed then there would be someone to make sure things went the way I'd planned. I was grateful for that confirmation. It literally felt like a ton of bricks had been lifted from my chest.

"Now!" he said loudly slapping his hands on his legs and standing. "Can we eat some food right now?" And just like that we were done. The conversation was over and I had a connection that ensured the safety of me and my girls. I wasn't for sure how getting in bed with these men would play out in the end. At the present time I had no other choice but to ride it out.

Six weeks went by and business was booming as usual. We had no further encounters with Lutz or Oleg. I thought we'd been quiet enough. Amanda walked into the office with a smile on her face.

"I take it you have some good news for me?" I asked. She nodded her head pulling out our venue confirmation.

"I secured the venue. Miranda should be in with all of the decorations." She responded.

"I thought you'd hired a professional to do all the party planning." I said scrunching up my face. Anything GFE Inc. did had to be top notch. While Miranda was great at answering phones, I wasn't too keen on her planning such an event.

"Trust me," Amanda smiled. "She has this under control." I wanted to fly off the handle, but I kept my impulses under wraps. I wasn't sure why I had trusted Amanda to handle most of the administrative work for the Masquerade Gala, but I had. It was too late to change things now.

"I hope you're not mad," she responded with a look of concern spread across her face. "We have receipts for everything and we didn't go over budget. Look." She said pulling out the receipts and pointing to the amount of money they'd spent.

As a matter of fact they were under budget. That to me wouldn't be impressive until Miranda walked in and I was put up to speed on what they had planned. Usually I was all up in the business part of the company, but with daddy, Chantelle, Victor, and Ryan I wasn't sure if I was coming or going.

Miranda came in with her hands full and out of breath. "I have tons more things inside the van outside, but I just wanted to show you what we've come up with and a sketch of how it's all going to be executed." She said placing everything on the round table in front of me.

I listened to her and was surprised to know that very little had been purchased from the stores. Miranda had taken it upon herself to contact Chantelle. They'd been working nonstop making custom decorations for the Gala. Unbeknownst to me Miranda had a creative knack as well. Miranda, her two daughters, and Chantelle had come up with an amazing concept for the Gala.

We even had custom made masks and costumes. I was actually impressed. When Miranda pulled out the laptop to show me the setup I was blown away.

"You did all this?" I asked.

"With the help of Chantelle," she responded nodding her head. If the venue looked anything like what I was looking at on the computer screen our patrons were in for a treat.

"You ladies did a great job."

Miranda started to ask me something but stopped. I'm sure I knew it was in reference to Chantelle and that was a question I wasn't going to answer. Changing the subject I asked if she was coming out to the gala. She declined, saying she had something to do with her church.

I started to ask a few questions myself. Like, how could she go to church and work for our company. I decided not to question it. I didn't know much about religion other than people got offended when you questioned them about it.

"You're wondering how I can work here and love God," she said with a smirk spread across her face. I didn't respond. I chose to look at her expressionless.

Miranda had proven to be an awesome
employee and I wasn't in the business of
losing good people or offending people I'd
grown to care about. If I was good to her
she would definitely be good to me.

"I don't need a response," she
laughed, finding humor in what she knew
I was thinking. "The way I see it, God
doesn't make any mistakes. We are always
exactly where we're supposed to be. You
provided me with a job when no one else
would. Who knows maybe one day I can
be of service to you too. That's the way the
world works. We are built to help one
another."

I sat there listening. Most of what
she'd said went over my head. I didn't
know how what we'd had going on
pertained to God or His so called Divine
plan but whatever. If that was how she
could look herself in the mirror and still
do her job, then that was fine with me.

"Are you ladies hungry?" I asked
changing the subject once again.

"Starved," Amanda chimed in. I
laughed, she was always hungry. I

couldn't understand how she stayed so small. She ate like a 250lb man and never gained a pound.

"I knew that," I said playfully as I picked up my Chanel handbag. "Lunch is on me." I responded, heading towards the door with my two girls in tow.

We opted to sit at the bar due to a 45 minute wait for a table. We all needed a drink to wind down.

"This place is nice I've never been here," Miranda said looking around taking in the scenery. "The atmosphere is great."

I agreed. I'd opted for a posh little seafood restaurant for the young and sexy. The drinks were always good and the patrons were all potential clients.

"Isn't that Loretta over there?" Amanda asked, pointing at the woman I had yet to fire for her shitty services.

"I believe so," I responded scoping out the scene.

"Look," she said becoming excited. "It's that asshole that tried to have me locked up." She added becoming red in the face. It sure as hell was. Ms. Loretta was with Victor sitting nice and cozy in the corner of one of my favorite restaurants. I scoffed before I slammed my shot of Vodka motioning for the bartender to send me another.

"Should we go say hello?" I asked sliding off the bar stool heading towards the duo. Miranda grabbed my arm to stop me. I assured her I was only going to say hello. I needed her and Victor to know that I'd seen them there. I wasn't sure why she'd pretended to not like him the last time we were together but the cat was out of the bag now.

"We'll be right back," Amanda smiled, leading me to their table. They didn't notice us approaching them until it was too late. They looked like two deer caught in headlights. It was almost humorous to me. Almost! I knew attorneys were liars, but that bitch was working for me and she couldn't serve two masters. One being the dick and the other was my money.

"Heeeyyyy," I said making sure my greeting was extra-long and fake.

Loretta quickly glanced at Victor, who just sat back and shrugged his shoulders nonchalantly. She stumbled over her words as she made small talk.

"Hey Tawny, how've you been sweetheart?" she smiled nervously.

I laughed at her weak attempt at conversation. "I've been pretty good and yourself?" I asked. Before she could answer I turned my attention to Victor. "And Victor Chastain," I said pleasantly. "Haven't seen you around in a while, how are you, sir?" I asked.

"Quite well Tawny," he responded, with a smirk on his face.

"Oh you two remember my good friend, Amanda," I added, grabbing her arm pulling her closer to me. They both nodded their heads.

"Yes of course," he said, leaning forward looking at her from head to toe as he licked his thick lips.

"Well," I said louder than I intended. "We just thought it was only appropriate to speak. We'll let you two get back to your little lunch." I said hovering my hands over their meals. We turned to walk away, but I couldn't just leave things at that.

"Oh Loretta," I said, doing a 180 degree turn on my heels as I snapped my fingers and pointed. "You're fired." I smiled, strutting back to the bar.

"I'm not sure what you said to her Ms. Tawny," Miranda said, sipping on her glass of wine, but she looks like she just seen a ghost." Amanda and I started laughing as we looked over the menu.

What a rocky five months. I didn't know things could get so complicated in such little time. I looked at my employees and smiled. I was actually grateful for them. I never knew I could be a leader, but apparently I was a damned good one.

My phone began to buzz notifying me that I had a text message.

Loretta: I really need to talk to you Tawny. I can explain. This is not what it looks like.

I deleted the message looking over my shoulder to get a glance at Ms. Counselor. She was no longer sitting at the table, but Victor was there. He was staring at me with the same lust in his eyes as he always had. I mouthed the words *fuck you* to him, then turned my attention back to my girls.

Next thing I knew the pair were leaving the restaurant. Victor came up behind me placing his hand on the small of my back. I turned slightly frowning.

"You have a wonderful evening, Tawny," he said. "I hope to see you soon." I couldn't bring myself to respond. Instead, I shook my head. There was no part of him that would see me soon unless it was by accident. I waited for Loretta to say something, but she didn't. I guessed she was waiting for a response back from her text message. That was definitely was not happening. What a joke.

I didn't pay her fraternize with Victor and then pretend like she didn't know him. I guess that was one thing you could expect from a lawyer. Lies. I sighed, thinking about what was to come. Three more weeks and we'd be at the gala making GFE history.

CHAPTER TWELVE

The chemo treatments made daddy sicker than he was before finding out he had cancer. I questioned had he made the right decision in going through with it. He was even starting to look sick. He'd lost a lot of hair so he'd decided to shave it all off. His skin looked paler than usual and he was losing a ton of weight.

I hated seeing him look like that. It ate me alive. My mom was around more. I guess she had left her other husband to come back to daddy. That didn't come as a big surprise. She probably was just waiting for him die. She was like that. The first opportunity she got she was on it. I just couldn't believe that my dad was falling for it. I watched as he sat in the chair allowing the medicine to drip into his IV and enter into his bloodstream.

I stared off into space wondering what my life would be like without my dad. Despite, me showing a whole lot of affection all the time I loved him more than anything. I didn't bother him much like my siblings because I didn't want to worry him. He worked hard for everything he had and my repayment to him was to do the same. If he left I'd have no parents. My mother and I never saw eye to eye and I didn't plan on that changing any time soon. My dad was all I'd ever needed.

I felt his hand touching mine. "Hey daddy," I said, looking concerned. His eyes looked so lost and empty. He looked weak not just physically, but in spirit. "You ok?" I asked, rubbing his hand gently.

"I'm fine baby," he smiled. "Just admiring the young and independent woman you've become. I want to let you know I'm so proud of you." He said catching me off guard. He'd never said those words to me. He didn't have to. I wasn't the type that needed verbal affirmation. I could see that in his eyes when we spent time together.

"I know daddy." I smiled, feeling a sudden pain in my heart. I didn't like how he was talking. His words seemed so final. I'd hoped that the treatments were working and his cancer would go into remission. If there was some God up in the sky that made everything happen, I needed him to show up. I hated there was nothing I could do. My back was against the wall and I needed a miracle.

My eyes filled with tears, but I refused to allow him to see me cry. I excused myself heading out into the corridor. I stood there for a moment with my back against the wall. I breathed in through my nostrils exhaling slowly.

I was in some serious emotional pain. And yet I had to keep on moving forward. My siblings weren't cutting me or my dad any slack either. They were still asking him for money knowing damn well he'd have to spend a lot more money on medical treatments. Yet he was still taking care of them and their children.

"Ms. Sinclair," I opened my eyes to see one of the nurses standing in front of me. I wiped the few tears that had managed to escape and slide down my face. "Are you alright?"

I shook my head yes before walking away. I went into the restroom to get myself together before facing my dad. My phone began to vibrate.

"Hello?"

"Everything is in order for tonight." Lacey spoke happily into the receiver. She was beyond excited about the Gala. As much as I wanted to join in with her I couldn't. I was worried about my dad and if we would be able to pull off what I'd planned with Lutz and Oleg. Hell I didn't even know if they were going to show up. If they chose not to I was going to be back at square one.

"What's going on with you?" Lacey asked. I still hadn't told them what was going on with my dad.

"Nothing," I responded, trying to bring joy that I didn't feel into the conversation. She was not taking "nothing" for an answer. If she suspected something wasn't right, she would whine until she wore you down to find out.

"Something's going on with you," she said, pushing a little harder. I tried to get off the phone with her, but she continued on. Finally I blurted out the truth. Well at least the truth about my dad. I damn sure wasn't about to tell her about Oleg and Lutz. She wasn't built for things like revenge. So we had to keep her in the dark by any means necessary.

"Oh my God!" she shrieked. "Is there anything that I can do?" she asked. I told her that I was fine and we were at the hospital now getting his chemo treatment.

"I'm so sorry Tawny. Maybe you should take some time off." She added. That was completely out of the question. I had a business to run. Although I had a good team behind me that I really believed I could trust, I needed to be in the front and center.

"I'm fine," I assured her before making an excuse to get off the phone. I really didn't want to talk about my dad's condition with anyone. Not even him. I loved my friends, but I needed to have that situation left for me to deal with alone.

After I dropped daddy off at home, I headed to my own home to get ready for the evening. Pepper and Cyn were there waiting in my driveway. I had completely forgotten they were riding with me. I greeted them both with hugs and a smile.

Three hours later we were ready to go. I wore a flowing blue see through gown with Swarovski Crystals individually sewn on to it from head to toe. It was a form fitting gown that stopped just at my ankles. My mask was one of a kind. It covered ¾'s of my entire face and was baby blue with silver and white detail throughout. Small crystals outlined the outer part of the mask as well as the eyes. The top part of the mask swirled around my head creating a crown fit for a queen. The silver of the crown gave off a natural beauty that only that metal could provide.

There were white, blue, and silver feathers on the left side that spread out at least 5 inches from my face. My lipstick was dark and sensual. My hair cascaded down my back in curly blonde locks. I looked like royalty. I was royalty. I was the Queen of GFE.

Pepper and Cyn looked equally as elegant with a little less glitz and glamour. Their gowns were made of satin and were accented with feathers and crystals as well. Their masks were a little less detailed, but none the less gorgeous. The white limo pulled up and we were ready to go. My heart was pounding in anticipation as we made our way to the Gala, picking up some of the other girls. It was now or never. Never clearly wasn't an option.

I looked out the back window noticing the same white car was behind us as I'd seen weeks before. Maybe I was just paranoid. How many people drove white Fords? A whole hell of a lot, I was assuming. I shrugged my shoulders deciding to join in on the festivities that were taking place inside of our limo. The ladies had popped a bottle of champagne and were ready to party.

Chantelle, Cyn, Amanda, and I all made sure we sipped slowly and kept our minds on the game plan. The reasoning behind the party was more than just to market our organization. We had business take care of.

The limo stopped and everyone except the four of us piled out of the vehicle. Lacey looked back concerned, but I urged her to go inside to make sure everything was as it should be. She complied ushering the rest of the ladies inside.

"Alright," I started. "Does everyone know their positions tonight?" I asked making sure that everyone knew where they were supposed to be and what they were supposed to do. All of the girls acknowledged their roles by stating them one at a time. I smiled happy that we were all on board and ready.

"Ok! Now it's time to handle our business." I said before exiting the car. When we walked in I was blown away. The lighting was magnificent. Blue hues illuminated the venue, making it look elegant, classy, and sexy. The crystal fixtures left nothing to be desired. The table decorations were superb and the long drapes hanging from the ceiling gave the place a cozy feel.

The caterers had the place smelling delicious and there was an open bar for everyone to indulge. Things were looking better than I'd expected. I texted Miranda telling her how well she'd done. She was definitely getting a promotion, bonus, or something.

"Miranda and I did pretty good, huh?" Chantelle said, giving me a slight nudge.

"Good?" I said raising my eyebrows.

"Yeah good," Chantelle said, faking an attitude. Her personality had taken a turn for the best lately. I was really enjoying her company nowadays more than ever.

"No, honey you two did great!" I said unable to lie. We walked throughout the venue, placing the last few touches here and there before Amanda began greeting our guests. People were pouring in by the masses. I stood in the shadows watching the door as everyone who walked in. There was no sign of Oleg or Lutz unfortunately.

I felt relieved to see that Jesus and Luiz had shown up. They looked as if they were thoroughly enjoying themselves. They'd taken a liking to one of our younger girls. Maybe they'd be requesting our services soon. Two hours in and I was still lurking and waiting. I walked over to Chantelle asking her if I'd missed something.

"I don't know if they're coming," she said, seemingly as frustrated with the situation as I. We decided to go talk to Amanda when the two men showed up with two women on their arms. They had to have been their wives, none the less they were there.

"What the hell is that shit?" Chantelle said, scrunching up her nose. I shook my head irritated myself. I wasn't expecting a third or fourth party. However, this may have been our only chance. We had to figure out what to do to get the two men alone. Cyn walked over discreetly displaying two small vials she had in the palm of her hand.

"What's this?" I asked not sure what she expected us to do with what I assumed was dope. It had been a while since I'd gotten high and I really didn't want to start again.

"Just a little something to ensure those two won't give you any problems," she said, motioning towards the two German men that were making their way through the crowd.

"What about the other two that are with them?" I asked still pissed that they'd brought dates.

"Oh those two?" Cyn asked nonchalantly. "You worry way too much." She added before walking off. I was glad she wasn't concerned because I damn sure didn't want to add any extra enemies to the list I'd already accumulated. I had enough drama in my life already. Chantelle and I looked at each other both concerned at how the situation would turn out.

Moments later Cyn came bursting through the crowd with the two women on her arm. Chantelle nearly spit out her drink. Cyn was a very bold young lady. I didn't know rather to be angry or just go with the flow. I stood there looking from Cyn to the two women who had put a monkey wrench in my plans.

"Ladies, I'd like for you to meet my cousins Gabriella and Consuela," she said in her thick Spanish accent. Chantelle and I looked at each other. A large smile seemed to simultaneously creep across all five of our faces. I smiled shaking both of the women's hands, nodding my head towards Cyn. She was a sneaky, sly little character. I didn't know rather to be happy she was on my team or afraid.

I didn't know how she did it and I wouldn't dare ask. I didn't need to know. All that was important was that the plan was back into play. Things would go down as usual. I could only imagine what those two sadistic bastards had in store for those women. Little did they know they were now our prey. We, the "weak" had become "predators". Cyn rushed the ladies off before Oleg and Lutz had the chance to miss them. Things were going great. Life was grand after all. Cyn was back in a matter of minutes grinning from ear to ear.

"Didn't I tell you not to worry?" she asked smiling. I nodded my head, admiring her ability to make things happen. Amanda was done at the door and was now helping bring drinks to each table. Lacey had taken the microphone instructing everyone to take their seats to prepare for the GFE Inc. speech.

I made my way up the small makeshift stage and began to speak. As the words belted out of my mouth, I had the audiences' full attention. Cyn had made two special drinks for our very special guests. When I was done speaking everyone held up their glasses, toasting to GFE the city's newest "networking organization".

I watched intently as Lutz and Oleg downed their drinks like the pigs that they were. I smiled slightly as I watched my Mexican friends close in on our targets. I stayed close so I could see every move that they made. When I noticed the pair becoming a little sluggish, I decided to make my move. Walking over to their table I greeted them.

"So good to see you two," I smiled extending my hand. Although they weren't sure who I was they decided to give me a shake anyway.

"I'm sorry do we know you?" Oleg asked.

"Of course you do," I smiled removing my mask. "It's me Claudia." I responded, watching the expressions on their faces. They were surprised, but didn't seem too worried considering they were on my turf now. Maybe it was because they didn't know they were outnumbered.

The two burst out in laughter patting one another on the back. They began speaking in German. I could clearly see that they'd found it quite amusing what they'd done to me. If I'd had reservations before about what I intended on doing to them all of that went directly out the window. I fumed with anger at their blatant disrespect of me and my venue.

"I'm glad you're amused." I smiled motioning for Luis and Jesus. They sent two other men that I'd had no idea were with them in our direction.

"Is there a problem here?" the two men asked, looking at me then directly at the two men. I explained that there was most definitely a problem and I needed them removed from the premises. The men didn't put up a fight. They left quietly without anyone noticing. The plan worked out perfectly for me. In a few hours they'd find out just how perfect my plan was.

CHAPTER THIRTEEN

The two men were strapped to chairs in the middle of the warehouse. Their faces covered in what looked like tears and vomit. The smell was almost unbearable. Chantelle and I exchanged glances before heading over to the four Hispanic men who were in deep conversation.

"Tawny, my girl," Luis said, giving me a big hug.

"I just want to thank you so much," I said, knowing that without his help Chantelle and I would never have gotten our revenge. He replied simply by saying, anything for a friend.

Cyn came wheeling a cart from a side door with a smile on her face. After snorting a few lines I was feeling more alive and ready than ever. Chantelle didn't seem like she was missing a beat either. She walked over to the two men removing their blindfolds.

Their eyes widened. Lutz began to apologize for what he'd done to her, placing all the blame on Oleg. She wasn't hearing any of it. It was as if an unseen force had taken control of her. Before I knew it, she'd slapped the hell out of Lutz, sending a large amount of spit flying from his mouth onto Oleg's cheek. He screamed like a small child.

Chantelle wasn't finished. She was out for blood. I'd never seen her like that. I looked on in horror while everyone else seemed unfazed. I glanced over at Cyn who had a strange look on her face. *Was she smiling?*

"What are you just standing there for?" Chantelle said, looking back at me sweat dripping down her forehead. She'd been putting in a whole lot of work. I stood there unable speak. I was stunned. I didn't know that Chantelle could be so violent and ruthless. I'd always thought that I was the tougher of the two, but I was wrong.

Everyone looked at me waiting for my next move. I didn't know what to do my entire body was trembling. It was like I was frozen in time. I wanted revenge, but I didn't know it would feel like this. I wasn't prepared for it to look like this either.

Chantelle smacked her lips returning her attention back to Oleg and his buddy. She went to town on them until they were so worn out they couldn't scream anymore. She was huffed and puffed violently. I wasn't sure if it was from the adrenaline rush or the fact that she'd beaten, cut, and burned them for damn near two hours.

I stood there unable to peel my eyes from the scene. I was having an outer body experience. My life right then had to be a dream. When she was done, she dropped the leather belt she'd been using to lash them with on the cart.

"Don't look so worried," Cyn smiled on as Chantelle walked our way wiping the sweat from her face. She touched my arm, causing me to flinch. Taking a step back, she gave me this weird look. Her eyes were empty. She was void of any emotion. In seconds the warmth I'd always seen in them came back as she reached out to me again. This time I decided to keep still.

I bit down softly on my lip, avoiding eye contact with her. How could I have never known she had so much rage inside of her?

"It's alright Tawny," she said, rubbing my bare arm. "I did this for us. They will never be able to hurt us ever again." She smiled. I felt like she'd crossed a line that she'd never come back from. My friend was different. I didn't know what that meant for us. All of the thoughts that were dancing in my head were drowned out by two loud pops.

Everything moved in slow motion. My eyes widened as I watched the smoke from the gun rise and disappear into the air. I could hear the word no lingering in the air, but no one's mouth was moving. I

looked around trying to see where the
sound was coming from until I realized it
was me.

Jesus had shot both men in the
head. Their bodies slumped over still tied
to the rickety old chairs. I turned away
from Cyn and Chantelle as everything I'd
ever eaten or drank poured from my
mouth. When there was nothing left to
come out my body continued jerking
violently. I dropped to my knees feeling as
if I'd taken a blow to the stomach.

"I'm sorry Ms. Tawny," Luiz said as
his hand touching my back gently.
"They've seen all of our faces."

I couldn't say anything. I was
hyperventilating. Even inside that big
empty warehouse I couldn't breathe. The
walls were closing in around me. Beads of
sweat covered my forehead as my mouth
became dry. What the hell had I gotten
myself into? Who were these people?

I wasn't built for this. My high was
now completely gone. I wanted to run out
of there, but I didn't, for fear of being shot
in my back. What if they thought I was

going to tell? Oh my God, I was a witness! I was trembling so bad that I felt like my elbows and knees were going to collapse from under me.

"This happens to most people their first time experiencing something like this," Cyn said, leaning beside me. That bitch was crazy. I didn't want her working for me or with me. How in the hell was I going to get rid of her? Or did I really want to get rid of her? Clearly they had a strong network and I still had a problem. A very big problem, named Victor, who happened to work for the DEA.

Cyn and Chantelle helped me up and into the car as Luis looked on with concern. I still wasn't sure how to read his expressions, but I prayed he wasn't angry. The car ride was silent. I didn't have much to say. All of us were deep in our own thoughts. Chantelle had just tortured two men before they were killed. I was sure she was worse off than I, but then again maybe not. I exhaled as I leaned back closing my eyes.

In what seemed like seconds we were pulling up to my condo. I hoped that this was all a bad dream, but it wasn't. The smell of my own vomit and the thought of what I'd just witnessed caused me to gag. I was in for a long night. I planned on going inside the house and trying to get some much needed rest.

I stepped out of the car when my phone began to ring. I didn't bother answering it. Cyn walked me to the door asking if I needed her to stay. I was too drained to even respond. It felt like all of the life had been sucked from me. I didn't know what to do with myself. My emotions were all over the place. I was in a good, bad, and ugly place all at the same time. My phone started ringing again. Cyn looked at me confused.

"Do you want me to get that for you?" she inquired, grabbing my phone from my hand. "It says it's your dad." She responded, drawing me out of my stupor. My heart sank to my toes. I snatched the phone from her hands fumbling with it before it dropped to the ground. The phone shut off displaying a black screen.

"Shit!" I cursed aloud. For those phones to have been so damned expensive, they broke too easily. I picked it up powering it on praying that it worked. That was one thing that went right for the night. I held my breath as I called daddy back.

My mother answered the phone crying, I could barely hear what she was saying. I was becoming pissed. I wished she would just calm down so I could understand her. She was hysterical. I could feel myself sweating, although it was a cool 65 degrees outside.

Cyn looked at me as if to ask what was going on. I didn't know. I just handed her the phone. I didn't want to talk to my mother. I couldn't understand why she was with my father at this time anyway. She had ulterior motives and I didn't have the patience to deal with her.

"Hello, Mrs. Sinclair?" Cyn spoke into the phone. Cyn introduced herself and despite my mothers' current state remained calm. I could tell by the expression on her face that something was wrong. I wanted to know, but then again I didn't.

How was I going to be able to handle bad news about my father? I knew it was about him. My mother never called me and especially not this late at night. My heart pounded as my breathing became shallow and light. I closed my eyes breathing through my nose and out my mouth. I repeated those steps a few times in an attempt to calm myself. It wasn't working.

Cyn ended the call and told me we had to go to the hospital. I wanted to ask her why, but I didn't. I already knew why. I wanted to hold off on the bad news as much as possible. I was scared. For the first time in my life I cared if someone died. It didn't feel so natural anymore. It wasn't a part of life's process. Not when it pertained to daddy.

"What's going on?" Chantelle asked, seeming to be back to her old self. Cyn told her we were headed to the hospital. "Oh my God, is it Mr. Sinclair?" she asked. Cyn shook her head yes in response as she backed out of my driveway.

The entire ride was a blur to me. I didn't want to go to the hospital, but I didn't want to not be there for my dad either. I hoped that my siblings weren't there. After the night I'd had there wasn't any telling how I'd respond to seeing them. They were like vultures. Sitting there waiting for the prey to die so they could devour what was left. In daddy's case his fortune.

Cyn pulled up directly in front of the hospital doors to let me out. I didn't moving. My legs felt as if they would give out as soon as they hit the pavement. I didn't want to chance it. The two ladies in the front seat looked at one another before Chantelle helped me get out the car. I was more than weak, almost lethargic.

"It's going to be ok," she responded. I wanted to acknowledge what she said but didn't. I couldn't. When we got up to the receptionist at the front desk, she gave us a funny look.

"Do you need to see a doctor?" she asked looking mortified. For the first time we realized that Chantelle still had the Germans blood all over her. She looked like she belonged in a horror movie. Chantelle was quick on her toes, however stating that we'd just left a masquerade party that had gotten way out of hand. The receptionist seemed amused and didn't press on any further.

My best friend took control asking for Donald Sinclair's room. We were directed to the 6th floor. The elevator ride seemed to go on forever. With each ding my body flinched. The sound signified being that much closer to the moment of truth. Chantelle held onto me tightly. She knew that my daddy was my world. Other than my girls he was all that I had.

When the doors opened I immediately saw my brothers and sister hovered together. They looked as if they'd been crying. My sister Vanessa rushed over to me hugging me tightly. I reciprocated the hug, holding her like I didn't want to ever let go. It seemed like I melted into her embrace. I wasn't sure what had come over me, but there was feeling there.

I needed someone to understand what I was going through. I longed for someone to share the worry and pain I felt concerning my dad. Vanessa's embrace felt real. Or maybe I was just vulnerable. None the less I accepted her open arms as comfort and protection. As the tears flowed from my eyes, I breathed easily.

"He's not going to make it," Vanessa said through deep pain felt sobs. It was the reality I knew was coming. I had prayed and hoped for the best but why would God have listened to me? I felt angry and betrayed as I shook uncontrollably. My sister called for one of my brothers to come help her with me. They moved me over to a couch while someone went to get me water.

My mouth was dry, my head pounded, and my heart had broken into a million pieces. I wanted to say something, but couldn't. I had been silent the entire time with the exception of my sobs. I wanted to see daddy. The pains of life had its claws deep inside of my being.

The feeling was surreal. The elevator doors dinged as Lacey and Cyn rushed to my aid. We sat there waiting until my mom came out to give us an update. She looked relieved to see me. Believe it or not I was happy she was there. She grabbed my hand, telling me that he wanted to talk to me.

As we walked down the corridor, I had an eerie feeling. It was like I was in the twilight zone. Everything around me seemed near but distant. The closer we came to his room the further away I felt. My mother stopped at the entrance of his door looking me in my eyes as she ran her hand down the side of my face.

"With age come regrets," she started as tears strolled down her face. Her voice cracked. "I'm sorry I haven't been the type of mother that you needed, but I'm here now." She added, before hugging me and allowing me the time I needed to spend with my dad. I took a deep breath before walking in.

What I saw damn near killed me. I'd just left him earlier and I didn't recall him looking this vulnerable. He called out my name. He was so transparent I couldn't tell that he knew I was there. He could barely lift his hand, but he'd managed to reach out to me. I walked quickly to his side.

Tawny was almost back! I'd always played strong for him and although I was the weakest link right now I couldn't let him know I was afraid. I grabbed his hand, taking a seat next to the bed. He gave me a faint smile. I couldn't believe this was happening. I wanted to get up, jump up and down, having a tantrum, scream why at the top of my lungs. Why my father?

"Did I ever tell you about the day you were born?" he asked catching me off guard. I sat there stuck in my own thoughts until he faintly squeezed my hand awaiting my answer.

"No" I mustered weakly.

"I missed that moment," he said. I could feel the guilt that poured from his being. "When I got here, to this very hospital and saw your beautiful face," he said, smiling, "I vowed to never miss another day of your life."

Tears strolled down my face. I didn't know why he was telling me this. Like he said he vowed to never miss another and he hadn't. He'd always been in my life.

"Your mother never forgave me for that," he laughed. "I wasn't the best husband you know?" he admitted.

"But you were the best dad," I whispered, rubbing his fragile hand.

"The best dad wouldn't have been cheating on his wife while she was giving birth to his child." He sighed. "Your mother loves you." He added before he went into a fit of coughing as blood spewed from his mouth. I tried to help him, but I couldn't.

"Nurse! Nurse!" I screamed before hitting the red button on the bed and running out the room. That was the last conversation I'd ever had with my dad.

CHAPTER FOURTEEN

Ryan sat with his arm wrapped around my shoulder as I stared out into space. The house was filled with people, who'd come to grieve with us. My dad was a popular and well respected man. My father had impacted many lives during his time here on earth. He was a pillar of the community. So many people came forth to speak at his funeral about the awesome things he'd done for them. I couldn't have been more proud to say he was my father.

Even Victor showed up to give his condolences. I guess I shouldn't have been surprised. He was one of my daddy's "best friends".

"I'm looking for Tawny Sinclair," I heard an unfamiliar voice say. I didn't bother to look up. I heard someone else pointing him in my direction.

"Tawny Sinclair, can you stand up please? You need to come down to the station with us..." everything else was blur this could not have been happening to me. On the day I buried my father! Really?

I could hear my mother asking what was going on. She became hysterical screaming for them to take their hands off of me. I couldn't even look at her. I couldn't face anyone. I could hear the patrons whispering as I was escorted out of the family home by two officers.

My mother walked briskly alongside us telling me to keep quiet. She'd become extremely aggressive, to the point that one of the officers threatened to arrest her. That didn't stop her from telling them they'd be hearing from our lawyer. I was numb to what was happening around me. I didn't even care at that point. What was a lawyer going to do? Hell, I didn't even know what I was being questioned for. I was sure I'd be out sooner than later. I hadn't done anything wrong.

I chose to hitch a ride to the station in the police car. I sat silently waiting to face whatever was coming my way. I knew it had to be something Victor had put together. He was such a sneaky bastard, pretending to be someone we could trust. My jaw became tight as I thought of all the things I would say to him once I got home. I'd had it with all the nonsense that was going on in my life. When was all this shit going to end?

They put me in a room by myself before two plain clothes officers entered introducing themselves. I'd watched enough movies to know that one would be playing "good cop" and the other "bad". I didn't say a word. I'd just buried my dad three hours earlier and here they came with this crap! I asked what was going on.

"We wanted to ask you some questions about a missing person's case," the woman said, causing me to frown. I didn't know shit about any missing persons. They'd come to my home on the day I lay my father to rest about a missing persons case?

The female officer threw several photos of Oleg and Lutz onto the table in front of me. I was nervous as hell. I wanted out of that room and fast. How in the hell did they connect me to that shit? My heart skipped a beat, but I kept my game face on. I pretended as if their faces didn't mean a thing. I needed my lawyer, ASAP. I tried to remain calm as visions of their brains being splattered all over the warehouse invaded my mind.

"Do you know these men?" the female cop asked with too much attitude. I looked at her as if she were crazy.

"What is this about?" I questioned through squinted eyes. I wasn't going to answer a thing. Every question they asked was going to be answered with my own question.

"You know exactly what this is about," she said, seeming to become angrier just by looking at me. I scrunched up my face looking confused.

"I'm sorry Officer Gordon, but if I knew I wouldn't have asked." I responded pretending to be oblivious to the fact that these two men were missing. What they didn't know was that they were dead. As long as they were missing and they didn't have any evidence suggesting foul play in their disappearance they didn't have anything on me. Judging by the thoroughness of my Mexican friends, I was clean and clear to be free.

"These men were last seen talking to you at some big extravagant ball you were throwing for..." she sifted through a stack of papers. "GFE Inc. a prostitution organization that you own." She said with a disgusted look on her face.

"Prostitution?" I responded looking at her as if she was bat shit crazy. Before I said too much, I stopped, sighed, and asked for my lawyer. Officer Gordon slammed her hands onto the table continuing to talk about shit she knew nothing about. She was starting to get on my fucking nerves. Today was not the day for me to deal with this. I prayed either my attorney got there pretty quickly or "good cop" chimed in or I'd be facing assault charges on a law enforcement officer. I literally wanted to kick her little scrawny ass.

I took a deep breath before asking her politely to get out of my face. She wasn't letting up, however, until "good cop" finally stepped in. I clenched my jaw, staring her down as he began to speak to me in a gentle manner.

"We just need you to answer a few questions," he said softly hoping I'd bite. I wasn't answering anything. From what I'd known about the law they needed to leave me the hell alone after I asked to speak with my lawyer. Then again, maybe I was wrong.

"I want my lawyer," I sighed leaning back in the chair. There must've been a group of angels surrounding me because before they could say anything else Loretta burst through the doors. I was both relieved and pissed to lay eyes her. I hadn't seen her since I fired her. She jumped into action handing the two officers their asses.

"So is she under arrest?" she asked. The officers shook their heads in unison. "Okay so she's free to go?" she said motioning for me to stand.

Officer Gordon wasn't going to give in that easily. She stated that they had the right to detain me for up to 48 hours and they may exercise that right.

"Are you kidding me?" Loretta asked, making a face. "What is this about?" she asked. Officer Gordon went on to explain that I could be involved in a serious crime. I rolled my eyes as she spoke with Loretta.

"Good luck with your investigation, but my client is going home now until you charge her with something," Loretta stated causing a look of confusion to spread across the officers' faces.

"And why is that?" the evil bitch of a cop asked sarcastically. Loretta motioned for the two cops to meet with her outside.

I sat there waiting for what seemed like hours before they returned. Loretta advised me to get my things we were leaving. I sighed with relief. I didn't know how she did it, but I was glad she did. As we walked down the corridor, I heard a familiar voice. I turned to see Victor speaking with someone.

"She just lost her father. I can assure you that she had nothing to do with the disappearance of anyone." He responded. "The night in question I was with her supporting the launch or her business." I could hear him say. He was really putting his ass on the line for me. Why? I knew there was something behind the madness.

"Come on," Loretta urged tugging at my elbow. I hesitated before following her out of the precinct. When we got in her car she let me have it despite the fact that I was still pissed at her.

"What the hell is going on Tawny?" she yelled, as we peeled out of the parking lot.

I sat there quietly. I still didn't know what side, she was on. I didn't trust her. She'd lied to me before and I wasn't taking any chances with her now. I stared out the window only offering a simple thank you for her help.

"Listen," she said sighing. "I didn't tell you about Victor and I, because we like to keep our relationship under wraps." She stated. That didn't do much for me however. I wasn't sure of the extent of their relationship I just couldn't deal with liars.

"Tawny," she started placing her hand on my knee. "You know what kind of man Victor is. As long you give him what he wants, he'll make sure any problems you might have will "go away"." She said stating the truth. "How in the hell do you think I'm able to win cases the way I do?" she asked causing me to think long and hard.

Loretta always had information that could only be given by an inside source. A smile crept across my face as I allowed my guard to be let down slightly.

"You see, sweetheart," she began. "Sometimes it's not what you know it's who you know. We all have to scratch each other's backs. Even when it means sleeping with the enemy," She stated, all too knowingly. I fully understood the extent of their relationship. I couldn't be mad at her about it, but I was curious about what Victor would want from me.

"And what do I owe Mr. Chastain in return for this... Favor," I asked knowing that there was more to the story than what met the eye.

"A piece of GFE," Loretta responded with a sigh.

"Hell no!" I said, pissed that she'd even called him. Sure an alibi from the DEA was perfect and would get me out of the shit I was in, but he wasn't getting shit from me. Had it not been for him I wouldn't be caught up in any of this mess to begin with.

"Tawny, you're smarter than that," Loretta said, glancing over at me before putting her eyes back on the road. "You know what he's capable of doing."

"I don't give a damn what he's capable of doing!" I said, expressing my anger for Victor towards Loretta.

She sighed in frustration asking me what my problem was with him. Although I didn't really trust her either I was feeling vulnerable so I let her in on our little secret. She sat there silent for what seemed like an eternity.

"Well don't start speaking too soon," I said sarcastically, breaking the silence. She apologized, but advised me that maybe I could use this whole issue to my advantage. I looked at her as if she was crazy. How in the hell was I going to take advantage of this situation?

"I know this sounds crazy, but what if you gave him one more chance?" Loretta suggested. If looks could kill I'd be trying to regain control of the steering wheel, because Loretta would be long gone. "It's not what you think." She said holding up her hands.

"Then what could it possibly be?" I asked uninterested, however the more she spoke the more liked what she'd had to say. I could see why she'd always been the family attorney. She was smart. She knew how to play her cards right. Most of all she was a barracuda.

"So when do we get down to business?" I asked, ready to get back into Victors good graces.

"There's no greater time than the present." She responded, with a smile spread across her face. She was absolutely right in saying so. I'd done too much to turn away. I needed Victor more now than ever. I couldn't end up going to jail. I didn't even know how the cops came to find out about me, the gala, or those broken English speaking bastards, in the first place. My circle was tight. Everyone involved had something to lose and nothing to gain. Or did they?

"Do you know who told them that I was involved with the disappearance of those men?" I asked picking Loretta's brain.

"According to Victor, they got an anonymous tip and some pictures of you with them at your event." She responded. My mind ran rapidly as I wondered who could've been taking snapshots at my event.

Loretta dropped me off at my father's house. My mother had managed to clear almost everyone out of our home. When I walked in I found her in the kitchen sobbing. She'd left the station long before they let me go, with Loretta assuring that I'd be home soon. I placed my hand on her shoulder, squeezing lightly.

"I don't have him anymore and I can't lose you too," she sobbed embracing me tightly. That numbness had presented itself again. This time instead of being strong for my dad, I knew I had to be strong for my mom. I'd now become her protector. It was a trait that was just in me.

"It's going to be alright mom," I responded, catching her off guard when I didn't refer to her by her name Elizabeth. "It was just a misunderstanding." I added lying through my teeth. I couldn't tell her the truth. I wasn't sure if she'd understand. She cried stating that she hoped so.

Chantelle took it upon herself to clear out the rest of our guests. We needed some time to deal with family business. Even my brothers and sisters respected the fact that my mother and I needed to be alone in this process. Out of all those years of bickering and fighting amongst one another I was amazed at how easily everyone was able to come together. Typically in situations like this there'd be more chaos than ever among families. Not this one. Maybe we were a lot closer than I'd believed us to be.

CHAPTER FIFTEEN

"Tawny, it's so good to see you back!" Miranda loathed as she gave me a huge hug. "I've been praying for you." She added, before stating the reason she hadn't called was because she knew I needed time to grieve. I smiled, thanking her for everything she'd been doing. Miranda and Amanda had managed to run GFE Incorporation alone for the past several weeks.

They'd been working closely with Lacey and Chantelle recruiting and booking nonstop. From the looks of things business was better than ever. Pepper was still working for me, but I hadn't heard from Cyn in a while. To be honest, no one had really heard from her. Pepper said she'd sent a few text messages to her but hadn't gotten a response. I hoped she was okay. Although I'd questioned her friendship before, during and right after my daddy's death she was right there. I knew there was loyalty in our relationship.

I had used my time off to get back into Victors good graces. Things were turning out better than I could've ever imagined. We had yet to discuss his interest in my business. However, I knew the day would come. In the meantime, I was prepared to keep him on a tight leash.

If there was one thing that would keep Victor at bay it was good pussy. Every chance I got I'd give him some. The first time I'd taken him back down memory lane I knew that I had him wide open.

"Hey Tawny," Miranda yelled from the front of the office as I sifted through some paperwork.

"Yeah," I responded.

"I need to talk to you about Pepper," she said. From the look on her face I knew it had to be something serious. Probably something I wasn't prepared to deal with on my first day back into the office.

"Can it wait?" I asked sighing heavily. I'd been dealing with enough.

"I think you want to hear this."

I gave Miranda my full attention. As the words escaped her mouth, I got an instant headache. I was right. I didn't want to deal with it. I asked Miranda to hand me her file as I went through all of paperwork with a keen eye. We had been so excited about our new celebrity client we hadn't paid much attention to detail.

"Fuck!" I yelled, throwing the manila folder onto my desk. Miranda stood there staring at me not really knowing what to say. "Thanks." I told her, pinching the bridge of my nose with my thumb and forefinger.

"What do you want me to tell them if they come by again?" she asked, looking concerned.

"Keep telling them you don't know her. If they decide to call the police then call me immediately," I stated, before grabbing my keys from the table to leave. I had to get out of the office. I was ready to shut the entire place down, say fuck the money and all. GFE Inc. was starting to become more of a headache than anything else. I called Ryan to see if he wanted to do lunch.

"Hello?" an unfamiliar voice sang into the phone. I looked at the receiver to make sure I'd dialed the correct number. It said Ryan so it had to be his number. She said hello again before I stuttered over my words asking for him.

"Who's this?" she asked harshly.

"Tawny," I responded, having no energy to exchange.

"I'm sorry Ryan is busy right now!" she yelled, before hanging up in my face. I was sick of this back and forth shit with Ryan. He was going to have to choose either me or whatever her name was. I didn't have the time or patience to compete for his attention. I wanted to call back, but instead opted to throw my phone into the passenger seat and get something to eat by myself.

Come to think of it, I wasn't too hungry anymore either. The closer I got to the restaurant, the more I wanted to go to Ryan's apartment. Sure I didn't need the drama, but I did need the closure. I made a U-turn heading towards his apartment. I didn't care if she was there or not. He was going to make a decision either me or her.

I'd come clean with him about everything. Well almost everything. He knew that Victor was blackmailing me, but not for what. I told him it was a sensitive matter that I was working on resolving. I didn't leave any stone unturned and he seemed to be ok with that. Well at least I thought he was. I was as honest as I could be with him without implicating him in my bullshit, and yet he was still dealing with that girl.

I didn't realize I'd been speeding until I heard the sirens behind me. I shook my head mad at myself for getting lost in my thoughts once again. That was happening a whole lot lately.

I pulled over getting my license, registration, and proof of insurance ready to go. After my last encounter with law enforcement I wanted to stay away from them as much as possible. I rolled down my window holding my documentation in my left hand.

"How are you doing today ma'am?" the officer asked. I mumbled fine never taking the time to look over at him. "I see not much has changed on the privileged kid side." He said chuckling.

I didn't know what the hell that meant and was prepared to tell him to just give me my damned ticket. He looked so familiar. I was trying to place where I'd known him from.

"Tawny Sinclair, it's me Derek Thompson!" he smiled brightly. How could I have ever forgotten about Derek? He was the nicest kid in school. People always bullied him, but never I, I liked him a whole lot. I remember I socked Ryan right in the nose during recess for calling him names.

His parents ended up dying in a car accident and he just disappeared. We'd heard he'd been put in foster care because he had nowhere else to go. No one ever really knew. I'd always wondered about him. It was actually good to see him.

"That would be me." I smiled, remembering a time in my life where things were a whole lot better. Being a privileged kid wasn't what I felt like at the moment.

"I can't possibly give the girl who kicked Ryan's ass for me in the 3rd grade a ticket." He said, as we both shared a good laugh. Little did he know I was on my way to kick Ryan's ass again.

"Thanks," I responded, smiling genuinely for the first time in months.

"No problem," he responded. "Just make sure you slow down Ms. Sinclair," He said before walking back to his squad car. That was a nice little turn of events. It had been a while since something turned out in my favor without some bullshit attached to it. That should've been my queue to turn myself around and go home.

I didn't though. I needed to talk to Ryan and the silly little girl who answered his cell phone.

When I got to Ryan's apartment, I could barely put my car in park before strutting up the stairs and banging on his door. I knew he was there because his car was outside. When he opened the door, I couldn't help but to try to slap his face off. He stood there looking confused and holding onto the side of his face as I brushed past him.

"Where is she?" I asked, walking from room to room in search of her.

"Where is who?" he asked, causing me to become more angry. Hadn't we been lying to one another enough? She'd answered his phone less than 45 minutes earlier and hung up in my face.

"Don't play stupid with me," I scolded. "She answered your phone and hung up in my face." I said, pissed that he was even trying to deny the fact that she'd been over there.

"Alexis?" he asked looking confused. Oh that was her name. Alexis.

"If that's her name," I stood there with my arms folded fuming with anger. He smacked his lips shaking his head as he apologized. That was it? An apology?

"How about an explanation," I said sarcastically. He sighed before sitting on the arm of the couch. I waited for it. I waited for Ryan to tell me the truth. I was prepared to slap his lips off this time.

"She came here to get her things it's over between her and I." he stated calmly. And he expected me to believe that?

"Where were you when she answered your phone?" I inquired, still pissed that he hadn't told me they still hadn't ended their "relationship".

"I was in the bathroom Tawny!" he raised his voice appearing to be annoyed by my line of questioning. I took a step back looking at him like he was a foreign object. This type of thing wasn't going to fly with me.

"Oh is my line of questioning bothering you Ryan?" I asked, pretending to be concerned about the attitude he was giving me.

Taking a deep breath, he responded by telling me he'd just had a long day. His long day compared to my long month wasn't shit. The year that had caused me excruciating pain was being compared to Alexis stopping by to get her stuff.

"I'm sorry for asking." I said sarcastically. "Let me just leave." I responded, feeling like I wanted to cry. Not because of Alexis but because no one seemed to understand what I was going through. Being raped and tortured, witnessing my best friends doing things I never thought possible, the sex, the drugs, it was all finally catching up with me. I rubbed my hands over my face before turning to walk out of the door.

"She's pregnant, Tawny," he said, sounding completely deflated. I had to blink several times as if that would help change what I'd heard. Did he just tell me that this girl he'd been seeing was pregnant? They'd been having sex unprotected? He trusted her and cared for her enough to do that?

My stomach turned at the thought that Ryan would be forever attached to Alexis. The bond that we had was no match for a child. I would never be able to compete with that. Who would want to? I stood there unable to move fighting back tears. I finally mustered the strength to nod my head and give him a weak smile.

"I don't want to be with her," he said, as if that would make me feel any better. I'd finally decided to be truthful to him and that was the thanks that I got. All I could say in response was *oh*. For me to have always had things so together these "issues", these "things" I continued to deal with were really beginning to take a toll on me.

I started to walk towards Ryan's door despite him begging me not to leave. I was suffocating in that apartment. I had to get out. I walked briskly to my car burning rubber out of the parking lot. Ryan hadn't even bothered to come after me. That was a good thing because I wasn't feeling quite like myself either.

I noticed the same white Ford that had been following me before in my rearview mirror. My heart thumped. What in the hell was going on? I made a couple unusual turns to be sure. Sure enough the car was right behind me. Despite the fear that was plaguing me, I decided to pull their card. I jumped out of my BMW at the next light throwing my hands in the air screaming, "*What!*"

I walked up to the car without even thinking. The windows were tinted so dark I couldn't see inside. The car started to back up before bolting straight towards me. I jumped to the side avoiding getting hit.

I ran back to my car jumping into the driver's seat taking off after the culprit. The old Tawny had reappeared. I wasn't the victim I was the victor. I don't know where the courage or strength came from but it was there. I swerved in and out of traffic until I was right behind the Ford.

It made a sharp right turn nearly hitting a pedestrian as she crossed the road. It was too late for me to make the turn, but I'd catch up. I hit the next right sailing down the main street until I came to a stop light. I cursed aloud hitting my steering wheel until I saw the lights of the police car.

Derek walked up to the vehicle policing! I slowly pulled into the parking lot adjacent to where the stop was taking place. I watched intently as the window rolled down. I couldn't see anything. He was blocking my view. I couldn't tell if it were a woman or a man. He walked back to his car I was assuming to run their information. The driver was leaning so far back in the seat I still couldn't make out who it was.

"Come on you son of a bitch. Let me see your face." I said to no one in particular. Derek returned back to the vehicle as he began to write out a ticket. The driver took the information before slowly driving back into traffic. I didn't see anything!

I needed to know who was in that car. I pulled out the parking lot tailing the Ford. I made sure I stayed at least four cars behind. The vehicle pulled into a modest apartment complex. The car door opened and I couldn't believe my eyes. It was that prissy little bitch Alexis getting out.

I wanted to get out of my car to give her a piece of my mind. As mad as I was I should've kicked her ass, but something else caught my attention. I watched intently as the woman approached her giving her a hug and a kiss on the cheek. They exchanged words before they walked over to a black Infiniti Q60 Coupe.

I looked on in disbelief. That disloyal bitch! Over 20 years of friendship went down the drain just like that. I didn't want to believe it, but I was staring it right in the face. Maybe I was overreacting. I was confused. I pulled out my phone just to be sure.

Dialing her number I didn't get an answer. I cursed as my nose started to flare. I dialed the number again, still no answer. I knew she had received my phone calls because I watched her as she looked down at her screen. I texted her stating there was an emergency. I watched for another fifteen minutes before driving off.

I called Chantelle asking her to meet me at Sebastian's Lounge. She declined until I specified that there was an emergency. Ten minutes later we were face to face as I spilled the beans about what I'd witnessed.

"I'm sure it's just a misunderstanding," Chantelle said nonchalantly, pissing me off even more.

"Then why didn't she answer my phone calls?" I asked. Chantelle admitted that I'd had a point. Pulling out her own cell she called Lacey, who answered on the first ring.

"Hey, where've you been we've been trying to get in contact with you?" Chantelle asked. I stared at her as she responded with a series of mm's, ok's, and ah's. I felt as if I was damn near going to fall out of my seat waiting to hear what Lacey had to say. Their conversation seemed to last forever. When the call was over she flagged the bartender over to order another round of drinks.

"Tawny we have another fucking problem." She responded, giving me the eye and looking dangerous once again.

CHAPTER SIXTEEN

Cyn stared at me seriously. I was stuck between a rock and a hard place. I didn't know what to do. I felt betrayed, because Lacey had been my best friend since kindergarten.

"Tawny, you don't know what she's capable of." Cyn insisted, looking over at Chantelle. I sighed, knowing that she was right. Could Lacey have been the anonymous caller who'd turned me into the police? Or was she the one snapping pictures at the Gala? If so, how did she know about the plans we'd had for the Germans? My leg bounced up and down as I contemplated my next move.

"This doesn't only affect you," Cyn advised. "My uncles won't be delighted to hear about this." She warned. I had forgotten about Luis and Jesus. She was correct, they weren't anyone to play with. Had they found out about Lacey and Alexis following us to the warehouse, it would be a wrap for both of them.

"But we don't know for sure if she had anything to do that anonymous tip." I responded. Cyn sighed, advising me that it couldn't have been anyone else.

"Sometimes you have to let go of those people ties." Chantelle said emotionlessly. I understood completely, but Lacey? She'd always been the voice of reason. She wasn't like the rest of us, she was sweet and kind. That alone is what had me on the fence. She couldn't be who we thought she was.

"Before we make any sudden moves let me talk to her," I started. "You know see where her head is at." The pair agreed reluctantly. I was relieved to know that I still had time to right the wrong. I prayed that Lacey didn't have anything to do with any of this. Despite my gut feeling I wanted to believe that our friendship meant as much to her as it did to me.

I decided to cut my dinner date short with my girls and head over to Lacey's house. I needed to get to the bottom of her lies. We'd never lied to one another before why start now? When I pulled up into the parking lot I noticed the white Ford immediately. I sighed debating if I should knock on the door or not.

I had to know the truth. I got out of my car heading up to her apartment. As I prepared to knock I could hear voices. I decided to press my ear up against the hard surface, maybe they could answer my questions without even knowing.

"What if they find out?" I heard Lacey saying nervously.

"They won't," Alexis responded.

"Ryan's going to eventually know that you're not pregnant and..."

Alexis cut her off abrasively. "Listen he's not going to find out. I'm going to tell him that I had a miscarriage. Do you want to stay in that bitches shadow your entire life? This was your damn idea in the first place."

Lacey started to speak, but Alexis cut her off again, telling her either she was in or out. Lacey told her she was in then asked what's next.

"Bring down GFE," Alexis responded.

"How?" Lacey asked, searching for guidance like she'd always done. I was livid. I should've known that the first chance she had she'd betray our friendship. She was too much of a follower. I didn't know when she started to become envious, but she had.

Alexis told her to figure it out before unlocking the door. I slipped to the side and hid in the bushes.

"I don't care what you have to do to bring her down just do it!" Alexis said, before slamming the door behind her.

I lay in the bushes confused. She was going through all of that behind a man and a small altercation? She had a serious vendetta out for me and had brainwashed my best friend into settling the score. I waited a few moments before peeking out of the bushes. I should've called Cyn and Chantelle they seemed to be professionals in handling business, but instead, I knocked on Lacey's door.

I was too hurt to leave not without saying something. Needless to say, she was shocked to see me. She poked her head out looking around into the parking lot.

"Are you expecting company or something?" I asked, pretending to be oblivious to the fact that she'd clearly become my foe. She nervously shook her head, no.

"Then are you going to let me in?" I inquired. She laughed it off apologizing before opening the door for me to come inside.

"What's up?" she asked, avoiding eye contact with. I wanted to sock her in the face. What did she mean what was up? She hadn't been returning any of my phone calls. When we did speak, she acted funny. Now that I knew she was in cahoots with a woman who had become my arch enemy almost overnight I knew why.

"I was going to ask you the same thing," I responded, looking at her with a smirk on my face.

"What do you mean?"

I shook my head, chuckling a little before telling her that I was just stopping by to say hey to my friend. The unexpected knock at the door caused her to jump.

"Are you okay?" I asked. "Do you..... want me to get that?" I said, walking towards the door. She jumped in front of me saying no she had it. I nodded, standing there with my arms folded, waiting for her to answer.

She turned her back towards me rubbing her palms on the sides of her pants. She walked to the door slowly looking out of the peephole.

"Who is it?" she asked faintly. I could hear the person cursing and fussing from the other side of the door. She asked her who the hell else would it be? I knew the voice all too well now. Lacey turned to look at me. I gave her an, *I don't know* look before shrugging my shoulders.

"I-I-I'm sorry I think you have the wrong address," she stated. The woman at the door wasn't taking no for an answer.

"I have the right address Lacey. Open the damn door!" She looked back at me then at the door. I stood there smirking waiting for what was to come next. She opened the door and there we stood face to face. Our eyes were piercing through one another.

"Well, well," she said, letting herself in walking directly towards me. "What a pleasant surprise." She smiled, invading way too much of my space. I prepared to smack her, but Lacey intervened.

"Do you two know each other?" Lacey asked, pretending not to know about our heated past.

I smiled while Alexis gave a rundown of our past encounters. Before she could go any further I cut her off.

"But, you already knew that didn't you Lacey?" I asked. She stood there unable to speak looking from Alexis to me. I didn't have time for the bullshit. Lacey was not my friend and apparently never had been. I nodded my head all too knowingly before heading towards the door.

Alexis grabbed my arm telling me I wasn't going anywhere. I went to snatch my arm away, but it was like she had a death grip on me. I could feel my body becoming hot as my heart rate increased. My legs were feeling funny like they were going to give out. My mind raced as my body started to jitter.

"Let my arm go!" I shrieked, trying again to pull away from Alexis. She struck me across my face. Instead of hair pulling my hands took on a life of their own. They were balled up tightly, allowing my knuckles to protrude as I rained down one vicious blow after another.

I couldn't stop myself. It was like everything I'd hated about what life had delivered me was being pounded into Alexis' petite little body. She yelled out for

Lacey to help her. When Lacey rushed over to me grabbing me, I gave her what she had coming also. I was experiencing a rage I'd never felt before.

Alexis came from behind pulling my hair again. I reached back grabbing hold of her head flipping her over my shoulder. She hit the ground with a thud. She lay there unconscious, bringing me back to reality. Lacey had slid into the corner looking afraid.

I stood in the middle of the room with my fists curled into tight balls as my chest rose up and down. For a moment all I could hear was myself breathing. I looked around noticing that in such a short amount of time we had torn the apartment up. I looked over at Lacey hatefully. I planned on laying her out too, until I noticed her pointing.

I followed her finger back to Alexis and my entire body deflated like a balloon. My shoulders slumped over as I fell to my knees. Alexis' neck was twisted in the most unnatural way I'd ever seen. She looked like she'd experienced an exorcism. I had done that. In self-defense, but none the less this was the result of something I'd did.

"We need to call the police," Lacey whimpered, from the corner with her cell phone in hand. I snatched the device from her slamming it on the ground. I stomped it four times as hard as I could crushing it.

"Nobody's calling the police," I said, looking at her intently. I went on to tell her I knew what she had going on with Alexis. Lacey's eyes grew big with fear. Those puppy dog eyes would get me every time except for this one. She was out to ruin me. Why? I wasn't completely sure. If I asked her I doubted she'd ever tell me. I wasn't even sure if I wanted her to.

I pulled out my phone calling Chantelle telling her to get over there quickly. She was still with Cyn, which was a good thing because she had all the connections. I waited for what seemed like forever.

Finally there was a bang at the door. I looked back at Lacey, who was still hovering in the corner weeping like the coward she was. I looked out the peephole it was two police officers. I ran over to Lacey pulling her to her feet whispering for her to help me move Alexis' body. We tugged at her motionless body as the two officers banged on the door another time this time identifying themselves. The banging became more intense, just as we got Alexis' body into the bedroom.

I instructed Lacey to get cleaned up. The blow to her nose had caused blood to drain from it. She hurried to do as she was told while I quickly slipped out of my clothes. I was down to my bra and panties by the time the men started jiggling the door knob. I slung the door open poking my head outside.

"Is everything alright ma'am?" One of the officers said, noticing that I was out of breath, and trying to peek inside the door. I didn't want them looking inside it was a mess. Moving my hair from my face and pretending to cover my breast I answered with a simple yes.

They weren't having it though. They looked at me intently stating that there had been some noise complaints.

Someone had called stating that they thought their neighbors were fighting. I shook my head no as if I didn't know what they were talking about.

"So there's nothing going on in here?" one responded, trying to look past me again. I needed to get them out of there and fast. The longer they stayed the more their chances of coming in and finding Alexis' body became.

I had to think fast. I exposed my nipples slightly as I made myself more visible in the moonlight. I could tell the two were becoming either aroused or uncomfortable.

"I'm so embarrassed," I laughed bashfully. "My girlfriend and I were having rough sex and sometimes things get out of hand." I added exposing more of my body and biting my bottom lip. I looked down at their pants both of them were definitely rising to the occasion.

Clearing his throat the short stocky one of the two asked if they could see my girlfriend to make sure she was ok. I called out for Lacey to come to the door.

She clearly didn't want to be stuck down at the station either, so she was on board. She came out only wearing a pair of thongs.

The officers looked at each other before apologizing and making their way back to their car. I closed the door leaning my back against it exhaling. As the breath exited my lungs I slid down one inch at a time relieved to have escaped the bullshit one more time. I looked over at Lacey, who was just as relieved as I was.

Twenty minutes later Cyn and Chantelle were at the apartment, taking in the scene that had unraveled. Cyn nodded her head in approval asking if I'd done all that. She was most definitely crazy, but reliable.

"So what do you want to do with her?" she asked motioning towards Lacey. I really didn't give a shit what she did with her. I didn't want her anywhere near me. If we let her go there was no guarantee that she wouldn't talk. Although she'd kept her mouth shut then she wasn't built to keep secrets like this. She was a slithery ass snake who couldn't be trusted. I said all of those things directly in her face.

"I won't say anything!" Lacey said, anxiously hoping to get out of the fiery pit she'd placed herself in.

"Oh bitch please!" Chantelle responded, throwing her hands up in the air. "We thought you could be trusted before and look what happened."

She begged and pleaded on deaf ears. Cyn called her connections to come "clean up" the mess I'd made. I had other business to tend to so I opted to leave. I was sure things would get handled appropriately.

Lacey begged me not to leave her with them. She was as unsure of her fate as I. My girls were pretty cut throat. Me on the other hand, I had a soft spot. What I didn't know I couldn't feel guilty or bad about. Out of sight, out of mind and that was how I had to keep things in dabbling in this business.

I drove to my condo to find Pepper sitting on the stairs.

"What now?" I mumbled noticing that she had tears cascading down her face. If it wasn't one damn thing it was another. I prepared myself for the worst.

When I got to her she flew into my arms hugging me tightly. I motioned for her to come inside. Anyone could be watching at any time. When we got inside she laid everything on the table. Most of what I already knew.

"I'm a minor!" she blurted out sobbing uncontrollably. "I ran away from my foster home a long time ago. Cyn and her family took me in. My foster parents.... They were abusing me. I couldn't take it. They didn't care about me they were only in it for the money!" she yelled out emotionally.

I knew she was a minor because her foster parents had come to my office looking for her. From what we knew the state was going to cut the family benefits off for her and charge them with her disappearance. I would've never hired her had I known she'd be bringing unnecessary heat to my business.

"Pepper you have to go home sweetheart. I can't have this kind of heat coming down on me." I responded. I wanted to be angry at her for not being upfront in the first place but she had to live. I didn't know her life so I couldn't judge it.

"I can't Tawny," she sobbed. "You don't know what it's like." The pain this girl felt pierced through my soul. I sighed before embracing her tightly.

"You can sleep here tonight, but in the morning we're going to have to figure something out." I said before heading to my room for some much needed rest.

CHAPTER SEVENTEEN

"No those terms are non-negotiable." The woman with the yellow teeth and the lopsided wig stated. I rolled my eyes. She didn't have a leg to stand on when it came to determining if something was non-negotiable. I let her plead her case however. When it was all said and done she would be leaving exactly the way she came with nothing.

That one night turned into three weeks that Pepper had been staying with me. I was harboring a runaway. If they caught her in my home or even knew that she was there I'd be digging myself out of more shit. I blocked the woman out as she went on and on about nothing. The more she talked the more she pissed me off. I had grown to love Pepper. She wasn't working for me anymore, but she'd gotten a better piece of the pie anyway. She and Magik had grown extremely close. Although she was under aged 16 years old, he was only 18 so it worked out fine.

Cutting the drug addicted woman off who was sitting in front of me I decided to speak. I couldn't take it any longer. "I'm at a loss for words." I responded, allowing a chuckle to slip from my mouth. She looked at me confused, showing me a frown of disapproval.

"And just what is that supposed to mean?" she asked in a raspy voice. That woman had to have been smoking since birth. Her lungs and vocal cords were shot!

"It means that I can't believe you two," I said pointing between her and the man sitting next to her. "Have the audacity to come into my office making demands after what you've put that young lady through." I could feel my face becoming hot and red. They both looked at each other the man becoming angry.

"Let me tell you something here," the man said, pointing his finger in my face. "I don't need no lily white bitch accusing me of shit." He nodded, acting as if he had told me a thing or two. I rolled my eyes yawning. They could bully anyone they liked with the exception of me.

"Well this lily white bitch will be calling the authorities on your child molesting ass." I responded seriously. "I'm sure you'll fair well from an investigation considering you stick your little nasty junkie dick in all the little girls that come to your home." My nose was flaring and I could feel my blood pressure rising.

"Oh bitch you don't know what the hell you're talking about." The man said, sniffing and looking around the room with bucked eyes.

"You're high right now." I stated calmly. "How about I call the police right now explain what's been going on and have you tested." I said nonchalantly picking up my office phone hitting 9-1-.

The woman leaned forward hanging up the line. She looked around as if she was tweaking, still trying to bargain. I wasn't having it, however.

"Listen," the woman said, leaning in toward me as if she had some sort of secret to tell me. "Just give us a couple thousand dollars and we'll figure something out." She responded.

"No but you can earn that couple thousand dollars." I said already knowing what I was going to say. The couple looked at each other anxiously.

"What you need us to do?" the man said with his Jethro looking ass. I ran down the entire game plan to them play by play. They sat there listening intently nodding along the way. "And that's all we gotta do?" he asked ignorantly.

"Yeah that's all you gotta do," I answered mimicking him sarcastically. The woman asked when they'd get their money. I told her as soon as the job was done they could have it.

I'd already spoken to Pepper about it and although she was nervous as hell, she agreed. I told her she had to trust me because I'd had yet to let her down. I wasn't going to start any time soon. Everything was working out according to plan. I jotted down the address on a piece of paper and urged them to get moving. Luring them in had taken longer than expected, so now we had to move fast.

I parked down the street in my rental watching the house intensely. Fifteen minutes later the two pulled into the affluent neighborhood, parking their 1990 Cadillac Sedan damn near in the yard. They got out the car looking like two sores peeking around the house and knocking on the door. No one answered.

I looked at the time it was 5:30pm. Just as I suspected one of the nosey neighbors had called 911. The couple ran to the car hysterically putting on a show that was movie worthy. They were screaming so loud that the officer could barely understand them. By the looks of it, he was on the verge of detaining them and taking them downtown. I prayed silently that they calmed down before they got arrested.

Here we went again. I knew better than to trust two junkies to handle something this serious. Then the woman shocked me. She took a deep breath holding up her hand and pointing to the home. I could hear her screaming, "She's in there, I know she is!"

"Who's in there?" the officer asked trying to figure out what was going on.

The woman took a deep breath before telling him. She said that her foster daughter had found a way to call her. She'd been missing for a while now. No one knew where she was at. She'd said she'd been kidnapped, raped, and held hostage by some white man! Just then Victor's car appeared down the street.

I slid down into the driver's side so I couldn't be made out. He hopped out of his car trying to figure out what all the commotion was about. The woman started screaming at him asking where her daughter was. She said she knew he had her locked up inside. Victor looked confused, wondering what in the hell she was talking about.

"Do you know who the hell I am lady?" he yelled, pointing his fingers and walking towards her. He was stopped by the police officer who'd called in for backup. The commotion brought out all the neighbors. They watched curiously as the dramatic scene unfolded.

Victor said he'd had enough of the circus that was taking place outside and was leaving. When he opened his front door blood curdling screams echoed throughout the house. The responding officer was on full alert pulling out his gun telling Victor to put his hands in the air.

"Please somebody help me," could be heard all the way down the block. The neighbors looked at one another. Then the whispering started. The more the screaming echoed throughout the neighborhood, the more pandemonium occurred.

When backup finally arrived, two of the officers entered the home with caution. Everyone watched from outside filled with anticipation. They returned with a beaten and battered Pepper. She was crying and had to be carried out of Victors home. The ambulance sirens could be heard in the near distance. Her fake ass foster parents ran to her aid. They hugged her pretending as if they'd missed her and were happy she was safe.

They had to slam Victor to the ground in order to get him cuffed. He yelled out he was DEA, but they didn't give a damn. He was going down to the station. I sighed one of relief. It was going to be a long time before I had to deal with him and his shit.

I'd spent the past several weeks working my way back into his good graces. I slept with him despite being repulsed by the act. I'd even given him a cut of GFE quenching his greedy thirst. He'd given me a key to his home and that was all she wrote. We'd come up with a plan to kill two birds with one stone. Pepper was the key. I'd slapped her up a few times, stolen some of Victors' semen, then tied her to the bedpost in his home after he'd left for work.

I knew her greedy foster parents would be on board when they found out what I had to offer. That saved their shitty lives and allotted them their freedom. When all of the commotion settled down I slowly drove off the block. I was free from Victor and his bullshit. The same way he'd ruined my life I'd done his except I was still standing.

"Hey Miranda are you ready?" I asked into the phone. She told me she was prepared to go. We headed to the hospital to check on Pepper. The police were questioning both her and her foster parents. Who we'd come to find out was her aunt and uncle. We waited some time before we were able to see her.

We didn't talk much about what'd happened. We needed to be as careful as possible with what we said and how we said it. There were eyes and ears all over the place. Nancy Gonzales the social worker assigned to Pepper's case walked in with a smile. She and Miranda exchanged embraces.

"Nancy this is Tawny," Miranda said introducing the two of us just as my mother was walking in. "And this is Elizabeth." She added, embracing my mother as well.

"It's very nice to meet the both of you." Nancy responded with a soft smile.

"I just want to thank you so much for helping this young lady," my mother said, walking over to the hospital bed and taking Pepper's hand. "She's just been through so much. And I know you went completely out of your way to do this for us, but we're so happy that you could."

Nancy expressed the concern she had for Peppers wellbeing which all amounted to one thing, our money. We spent a pretty penny in getting adoption paperwork expedited so that my mother would gain custody of Pepper until she was eighteen. Despite the fact there was an ongoing investigation concerning her foster parents and her whereabouts, Nancy had made some pretty impossible things happen. I guess that came with being "privileged". We could buy our way in and out of a lot of things.

I'd only agreed to help Pepper if she allowed me to help her. That included staying with my mother, going to school, and graduating not just from high school but college. I felt responsible for the predicament she was in. Granted she had problems long before she encountered me, but the truth of the matter was simple. She was my opportunity to give something back. She was the right to my wrongs.

She'd told me that she wanted to repay me for all I'd done for her. That was my solution to what she owed. I wanted her to survive. I needed her to survive and to become someone great. I needed her to be an inspiration to other young girls who found themselves in situations like she had.

My Mom was just as big as a piece of the puzzle. With daddy gone, we grew to really love one another. There were so many things about that woman I didn't know. To be truthful, I admired her strength and abilities to move forward. I never knew that she too had been a "paid girl". That was actually how she'd met my dad. I was unaware that she was half black. It was my daddy's parents who drove her away.

She looked at helping Pepper as her opportunity to not suck at being a mom. I knew she'd do a great job. She truly had changed a great deal.

"Thank you," Pepper cried.

"Aw what's wrong, sweetheart?" mom asked. My little friend was so emotional she could barely get the words out.

"Tawny saved my life." She responded. I smiled and exited the room quickly. I didn't want her to see me cry. I'd been doing a whole lot of that lately. To be honest, I needed her just as much as she needed me. Miranda walked out behind me placing her hand on mine.

"You ok?" she asked smiling. I shook my head yes knowing that if I opened my mouth, I'd be crying a river.

"It's funny, huh?" I asked

"Yeah," Miranda said, knowing exactly what I was talking about. We'd managed to show up in each other's lives at just the right time.

EPILOGUE

Amanda and I sat behind the glass with our bidding paddles in hand. The door opened, one by one the ladies filed in blindfolded and chained to one another. The sight took some getting used to, but business was business.

The three girls stood in front of us looking afraid and unsure of themselves. Amanda nudged me slightly as I continued staring straight forward. A large burly man pushed the first one forward. I looked her up and down and smiled. Lifting the paddle in my hand I placed my bid. I was content in knowing that no one else wanted her. I loathed at the fact that I would get to try her out before I bought her. I did this every time I came to the auction.

They removed her shackles as Amanda and I left the bidding room quietly. We entered the testing room prepared for the norm. She looked at us with wide, pleading eyes.

"The usual?" the man asked in a deep penetrating voice. We shook our heads yes and waited. Bad habits died slow. Although I'd learned a lot about myself and gained a lot of good qualities my thirst for revenge had never quite left. I watched as Lacey was viciously raped by two men. We looked on unfazed and unbothered as her screams turned into whimpers. Those whimpers soon became silence.

Once we were satisfied we left without the making the purchase. The same as we always did once a week. I'd come to the auction for the same thing. I'd never purchase any of those girls, but I'd watch Lacey suffer for her betrayal.

"So we're meeting up with the rest of the girls?" Amanda asked, leaning back in the passenger seat. I nodded my head as I pulled onto the highway. We drove in silence. Each of us lost in our own thoughts.

When I saw Cyn and Chantelle standing outside of the diner the feeling was bittersweet. Ironically this was where GFE Inc. was founded. It had been a while since we were all together and despite all the drama I'd had with GFE Inc. we were still going strong. Amanda helped me recruit an entirely new group of "Girlfriends".

Cyn had turned me onto bigger things. I had my hand in a whole lot of pots. It worked out for all of us. We each brought something lucrative and exciting to the table. Chantelle and Cyn had been doing a lot of business together lately. It seemed that their friendship had sparked a business relationship between Mr. Jackson and the Garcia Brothers.

That relationship brought our businesses to a whole other level. Cyn had finally proven to her uncles that she was capable of handling family business. They allotted her jurisdiction of the entire southeast region. She proved to be strong enough to withstand the tide because the crown had remained on top of her head for quite some time now.

Chantelle had finally come to terms with her father. He'd put her in charge of his "security business". She said she'd always dreamed of running that business. She never talked about what was secured, but she was clearly happy with how things were going. And I'd even utilized their services for my girls.

We all exchanged hugs before walking into the Cantina, together. They ordered drinks, smoked hookah, and enjoyed one another's company. Something caught Chantelle's attention on the screen, causing her to tap my leg. I looked intensely at Cyn who turned to see what we were staring at.

It was a picture of a Ms. Alexis Chastain the estranged daughter of former DEA Agent Victor Chastain. Her body had resurfaced in a river not too far from where we were sitting. They'd only been able to identify her from dental records. They were suspecting foul play and Lacey was the prime suspect. They also said she'd been missing for several months.

"Life's full of surprises," I mumbled under my breath seeming to be the only one surprised by the news. Amanda excused herself from the table leaving me open to ask questions. "Did you guys know about this?" I whispered to Cyn and Chantelle. They didn't have to answer their look said it all.

Cyn changed the subject beginning to make small talk. I guess some things were better left in the past.

"So, is Ryan ready for graduation?" she asked excitedly. I smiled acknowledging that he was. His hard work paid off and now he was graduating from law school. He'd be walking across the stage the following week Cum Laude. We were more than excited.

I sipped my virgin Pina Colada and smiled as Chantelle rubbed my small protruding belly. "And how's my little niece doing" she asked, just as the baby kicked ferociously. "Damn she's feisty just like her mama." She responded, snatching her hand back causing us all to laugh.

"I'm sorry I'm late you guys you wouldn't imagine the traffic out there," Miranda said, out of breath as she reached our table. "And this girl here, well we all know she's constantly busy." She added, pointing to Loretta who was right behind her in full lawyer attire. I rolled my eyes, knowing all too well.

"Where's my girl?" Cyn asked, looking around for Pepper.

"At home studying," I responded. "She has finals next week." I added. We'd gotten her a wonderful psychologist to help her sort through all of her emotional baggage. She'd been adjusting very well.

I looked at all the ladies that sat around the table laughing and enjoying one another's company. I was happy to have them in my life. We'd been through hell and high water for the past year and a half but it molded us. It brought us into the place we were supposed to be. No matter what the world would think if they found out half of our secrets, we were still valuable to one another. Miranda took out her camera causing everyone to groan.

"Oh come on you guys everyone squeeze in." She instructed. She needed a memory for every moment we had together. They all hovered around me smiling as she held up the camera with her selfie stick.

"Cheese," we all said, causing Chantelle to complain about how corny we were. Miranda snapped the picture and just like every other time we were together Chantelle was the only person with a frown on her face.

It didn't matter how things came together only that they did. Sometimes we'd find solace in the most chaotic places. There was a reason we were brought together. We completed one another. We could withstand the good and the bad. We were girlfriends with real life experiences and we'd always have each other's backs.